PUTTING THE PIECES TOGETHER

Putting the Pieces Together

Humberto M. Sotomayor

© 2025 Humberto M. Sotomayor

Published by:
Humberto M. Sotomayor

First Edition: November 2025

Certificado SafeCreative:

2511093639704-4DTKQA

Translation: Rosa Pugliese — www.rosapublishing.com

Cover Design: Daniela Álvarez

Digital ISBN: 979-8-9930902-3-8

Print ISBN: 979-8-9930902-4-5

Hard Cover ISBN: 979-8-9930902-5-2

Printed in the U.S.A.

PUTTING THE PIECES TOGETHER

Humberto M. Sotomayor

To everyone who has ever felt different,
out of place, out of this world:
You're not —you are unique,
you are special.

*"That simple beauty was still bearable barely,
and that if I live moment to moment,
garden to the stove, to the single act of flying,
I could have peace."*

— Peter Heller, *The Dog Stars*

Prologue

Toby sleeps in his small bed by the living room window, breathing deeply with a calm that always reminds me that life can be simple too. The floor lamp casts a warm glow over the armchair where I sit, a magazine open across my lap. The paper is heavy, rough along the edges, and still smells of fresh ink, as if the article had been printed just for me.

The headline fills half the page: "Matthew Prescott: the new voice of Texas architecture." I read it quietly, caught between pride and unease. Pride because I know what it means for the firm to appear here—doors opening, trust being built with clients who don't yet know us. Unease because I've never liked being the focus of attention. I'd rather let my work speak for itself —not the words.

There's a photo of me right beside the headline. The photographer kept asking me to smile, and finally I gave in. Now I look at it and barely recognize myself—not quite serious, not quite smiling, caught somewhere in between, as if uncertain of the man being portrayed.

Just below the image, a caption highlights the profile: "The architect who turns structures into experiences." I repeat it in my mind, almost under my breath. It sounds good—too good. Almost as if it were about someone else.

I turn the page carefully; the rough texture of the paper pulls me back to the present. The interview doesn't begin with me; it begins with Allison. I recognize her in every line—her quick rhythm, her way of sidestepping seriousness with a spark of wit. "Matthew has an almost childlike obsession with light," I read, and smile in disbelief. Only she could say something like that in a magazine.

She is described as the indispensable part of Divergent Holdings, the strategist who balances my chaos. And they're right. Sometimes I think Allison takes more pleasure in seeing me squirm with embarrassment over these articles than anything else. I can almost picture her laughing as she agreed to the interview, knowing I'd read every word with a frown.

Later in the article, Samuel appears—technical, precise, as always. He talks about calculations and tolerances, about how "Prescott pushes limits without breaking them." It surprises me to see him here, his name printed next to mine. I think that's the photo they should have used: not my uncomfortable face under a photographer's lens, but the three of us in the meeting room, surrounded by coffee-stained blueprints and debates that finally yield solutions.

I keep flipping through the pages. Photographs of our most well-known works unfold—glossy renderings that feel more like a dream than reality. The ink carries a scent of promise, as if the future could be captured on coated paper.

And yet, as I read each compliment, I feel that same familiar knot—that discomfort of reading about myself when all I want is for the work to speak for itself.

I leaf through the magazine. The photo they chose to open the article stares back at me: the immaculate jacket, the serious expression, the blurred backdrop of a rendering. "Handsome," some might say. I just think the jacket posed better than I did. That's not me—or not the version of me I recognize.

I go back to the paragraphs, the bolded lines, the phrases that seem eager to define me. The magazine presents them as certainties, but I read them as attempts to box in something that refuses to stay still.

The paper gleams under the living room lamp. Toby sighs from his corner, shifting slightly in his bed. I turn the page slowly, knowing that what follows is no longer someone else's words, but a portrait trying to capture me.

The first line of the article unsettles me. The title with my name is printed in bold, as if shouting—paired with adjectives that feel overblown. I lean back from the page, as though distance could soften the impact.

Below the image, a full-page photograph: me standing beside the model of our most recent project. The photographer asked me several times to look up, as if envisioning a promising future. In the picture, I look like someone planning to conquer the world. In truth, I only remember thinking the air conditioning was far too cold.

I keep reading. They praise my "breathing spaces," and talk about "an architect who turns the desert into a refuge." Big words, crafted to draw attention. I hardly recognize myself in them. What for me are hours of dust, doubt, and late-night revisions of a blueprint until dawn here sounds like a shining story.

The following paragraph circles back to Allison. Playful as ever, she offers her testimony. I picture her across from the journalist, smiling with that disarming calm, dropping phrases that sound spontaneous but always end up as headlines. "Matthew teaches us that architecture isn't just about constructing buildings, but about creating spaces where people can feel they belong."

I can see her saying it with that half-smile, secretly pleased to have slipped her voice into the story.

I flip another page slowly, as if they were fragile. The journalist keeps insisting on my achievements, on the "promise of a new era" and "the architect redefining the identity of the South." Too much noise. Words that feel too big for me—like a stiff, oversized suit just out of the dry cleaner's bag.

Then one more quote from Allison: "Matthew isn't someone who talks much about himself. His work tells the story." That line draws an involuntary smile from me. Yes, that's closer to the truth. She says it naturally, without embellishment. She always manages to say plainly what I cannot.

I close the magazine and set it on the coffee table. I stand and switch off the floor lamp. Toby lifts one eye, then drifts back to sleep, as if all this mattered far less than I imagine.

1 Divergent

It's past midnight when I finally look up. For the first time in hours, I notice how dark it is outside. Once again, I've skipped dinner. It happens often when I get lost in work.

On the main screen before me, the rendering of a new corporate building lingers, almost frozen in place. On the two side monitors, scattered notes and visual references wait patiently for my attention.

I lean back in the chair and exhale a long sigh. The office is quiet. Only one lamp remains lit, casting a gentle circle of light over my desk. I enjoy this silence. It's familiar, forgiving. I've always felt comfortable in it—perhaps because it never demands anything from me.

My eyes drift to the side table where I often sketch by hand. Some might call them drawings, but they're really just spontaneous strokes, messy lines that spill out without restraint. For me, they always make sense, though I doubt anyone else could read them.

I turn back to the screens. The building I'm designing matters; it's more than just another project. It has to carry the essence of Divergent Holdings—everything I am. It must be honest, authentic. It needs to convey something genuine. Maybe that's why I've spent so many nights here, obsessing over details no one else will ever notice.

The sudden vibration of my phone pulls me out of my thoughts. I glance at the screen instinctively. Of course—it's Allison. Who else would be texting me at this hour?

"Matt??? I'm sure you're still at the office! Tell me you ate the food I left in the fridge. Please head home; you need rest."

I can't help but smile. Allison has been my assistant for nearly seven years. But calling her that doesn't quite do her justice; she is my right hand, my external memory, and sometimes even my conscience. She's the only person who truly understands my chaos, though I still don't know how she endures it.

I quickly reply, trying to calm her even though we both know it's already too late.

"Not yet, Alli. I lost track of time. I'm almost done. I promise I'll leave in five minutes."

The message lingers on "seen" for a moment. I know she's pondering her next words, torn between the impulse to argue and the wisdom of just letting it go. Finally, she replies:

"Matt, your 'five minutes' always turn into hours. Please eat something."

I sigh, aware she's right. She always is. I must admit that without her, I'd probably be even more lost, missing meetings, birthdays, doctor's appointments—even meals. Yet, despite her efforts, I find myself hungry and lost in thought again.

I lock the phone screen and shift my focus back to the monitors. The buildings still stand there, gazing back at me, unfinished—a mirror of my own sense of incompleteness.

Maybe it's time to listen to Allison—at least this once.

The alarm blares relentlessly. I try to ignore it, as I do every morning, but then a small weight presses against my chest. When I finally open my eyes, Toby is there, paws firmly on me, looking as if he's been trying to wake me for hours.

"For God's sake, Toby, I'm up..." I mutter, my voice still hoarse from sleep.

I turn slowly toward the clock on the nightstand. It's ten in the morning. How did that happen? Once again, I stayed too late at the office. It's always the same: when I focus, time slips away.

I sit up and run a hand over Toby's head, silently grateful that if it weren't for him, I'd probably sleep until noon. Finally, I get up and head to the bathroom for a quick shower. I need it; otherwise, I'll never fully wake up.

When I step back, feeling more awake now, I head for the kitchen. Cooking is one of my favorite hobbies, but today I don't have the time. I grab the protein powder from the pantry, resigned to making a quick smoothie. As the blender roars, I look around. The counters are spotless, the cabinets are aligned, and the entire kitchen is neat and orderly. I know it isn't entirely my doing. Still, I'm grateful that someone helps me keep things in order—I can't quite manage it on my own, even though I love having everything perfectly arranged.

I chuckle to myself. A walking contradiction—that's what I am. I long for order and perfection, but I can't maintain them on my own.

I finish the shake quickly and check the time. I'm definitely running late. Back in the bedroom, as I sift through clothes, I pause, silent for a moment, reflecting on this daily reality. How can I be so competent in some areas, even "successful," and yet so utterly lost in others? An uncomfortable but straightforward thought crosses my mind. Allison's right: maybe I am a mess—more than I want to admit. And maybe... It's time to understand why I am the way I am.

The notebook I bought months ago to try writing is still there, sitting untouched on my nightstand. Maybe putting my thoughts on paper could help me sort out the chaos inside. Perhaps this is the right moment to start.

I glance at Toby, who is watching me from the doorway.

"What do you think, Toby?" I ask aloud, though of course he won't answer. He wags his tail, patiently waiting for my decision.

"Yeah, you're right. I can at least try."

I walk over to the notebook, sit on the edge of the bed, and open the cover, staring at the first blank page. For a moment, I hesitate, wondering what I should write first. I take a deep breath, pick up the pen lying on the table, and then begin, slowly.

"My mind never stops. It's always been this way. Since childhood, I've carried a constant noise, an endless inner dialogue that analyzes everything around me, as if my life were a film I must follow closely so I won't lose the thread. Some people think living like this must be exhausting, and I don't deny it; sometimes it is. But for me, it feels normal. It's all I've ever known."

When I finally make it to the office, Allison is already waiting at my desk, arms crossed, her expression caught somewhere between annoyance and amusement.

"Do you know what time it is, Matt?" she asks, raising an eyebrow.

"I know, I know—I'm sorry," I reply, setting my belongings down. "I stayed up way too late last night, and this morning I could barely get out of bed. When I finally did, I got caught up writing in that notebook I bought months ago. It's not like we had anything urgent, right?"

Allison sighs, then her features soften into a resigned smile.

"Not today," she says, "but don't make it a habit. Still, I'm glad you're finally using it. I don't know what miracle convinced you to start."

I'm just finishing my coffee when there's a knock at the door. I look up just as Samuel pokes his head in, watching me with quiet caution.

"Can I come in, or do you need a few more minutes to prepare yourself mentally?" he asks with a slight smile.

"Come in, Samuel," I laugh. "Don't be dramatic—you know I'm not that bad."

He steps in with a stack of documents under his arm and takes the chair across from me. Calm, talented, but too sensitive to criticism—Samuel has taught me over time to soften my tone, though I don't always succeed.

19

He places the papers on my desk: technical blueprints, new renderings I haven't seen yet. But before saying a word, he looks straight at me, taking a breath as if about to deliver bad news.

"Before you say anything, Matt, let me be clear: this time we did exactly what you asked," he says, half joking, half serious. "But before we go over it, I need to be sure you're in a good mood. Allison told me you were, though I wasn't entirely convinced."

I smile softly, raising both hands in mock surrender.

"I promise I'm in a good mood today. I even had breakfast," I say, exaggerating a little, though it's true enough. "Show me what you've got."

Samuel relaxes, finally smiling as he spreads the blueprints across my desk. I study each line, each image in silence, letting my mind imagine the building as it might feel once it's finished.

I like what I see. The team has captured the essence of our conversations—how this building should reflect who we are, our emotional core, and what Divergent Holdings wants to present to the world.

"I like it," I finally say, surprising even myself. "You really understood what we discussed—the balance between aesthetics, function, and feeling."

Since its inception, Divergent Holdings was founded with a clear vision: to stand out from the crowd. We don't just design buildings, spaces, or real estate projects; we aim to craft authentic experiences—places where people can feel a strong sense of belonging and truly connect with their surroundings. Each project is a reflection of our essence, our philosophy: that beauty lies precisely in what makes us different, in our divergence.

Samuel looks at me, relieved and almost disbelieving.

"Seriously? No changes?"

"Well… maybe just a few small tweaks," I admit with a grin. "But overall, this is exactly what we aimed for. Tell the team they did great work. And thank you, too, Samuel."

He nods, visibly pleased as he gathers the documents.

"I'll let them know," he says, standing up. "By the way, what's got you in such a generous mood today?"

I flash a quick smile, thinking about the notebook I began writing in this morning.

"Let's just say I'm starting to see things a little more clearly," I reply. "And I think that's good for all of us."

Samuel nods, not fully understanding but grateful that today was easier than most.

When he leaves, I lean back, staring at the empty spot on my desk where the blueprints had been just moments ago. Maybe writing is really what I need to find clarity in everything else.

As I gaze idly at the spot where the blueprints once lay, my mind drifts, as it always does, with a thousand thoughts vying for space. Then, without warning, a memory surfaces—sharp, vivid.

Senior year in Amarillo. I sat in the art room, working on a project assigned by Mr. Collins. I can still feel the pencil between my fingers, the way the tip bit into the paper, and that sharp frustration of not being able to put on paper what I saw so clearly in my head.

Around me, my classmates drew easily and confidently, as if it were the simplest thing in the world. I could hear their voices drifting across the tables, talking about weekend plans and small, ordinary things that seemed to belong to another life. I glanced at their drawings: clean lines, precise shapes, simple. Then I looked again at mine. My lines were crooked, imprecise, chaotic. But inside that chaos, I saw something beautiful, something unique. The problem was that no one else saw it.

Mr. Collins quietly sneaked up behind me. I knew he was there without turning around. He hovered over my shoulder, silently examining my sketches for what felt like an eternity.

"Matt, honestly, I don't quite understand what you're trying to say here," he finally said, his calm voice cutting through me like a sharp sentence. "Maybe you're overthinking things. Sometimes it's better to keep it simple so others can follow."

Simplify. The word echoed in my head as I tightened my grip on the pencil. Why should I change something that felt so clear and natural to me? Why alter the way I see things just because others don't?

"I'm sorry, sir," I murmured. I tried to mask the sting in my voice. "I'll try to make it clearer."

He nodded and walked away, unaware of how much his words hurt me. I gripped the pencil, my hands trembling slightly under the table. I wanted to run out, to escape that unbearable feeling. I felt exposed, as if everyone could see that something was wrong with me—that I didn't belong in that classroom, in that place.

When the bell finally rang, relief swept over me. I didn't turn in the sketch. I folded the piece of paper and pushed it into my backpack, carrying the frustration and sadness like a weight I couldn't put down. That afternoon, alone in my room, I tore the sketch to shreds, trying to erase the feeling of not fitting in, of being irredeemably different.

Now, years later, sitting in my office, the memory comes back with a bittersweet smile. That boy could never have imagined that the very difference he despised would become the foundation of everything I do. This building isn't just another project. It's my way—our way— of showing that difference can be just what we need.

I take a deep breath, letting the memory fade. The frustration still lingers somewhere, but it no longer controls me. I now see that simplifying was never my way.

The day has been longer than I expected. When I step inside, the familiarity of home wraps around me. The soft glow of the living room lamp and the quiet of silence feel like a warm hug. Toby waits by the door, tail wagging happily. I kneel to pet him, and he calms immediately, as if he, too, had been waiting for this peaceful moment.

"I missed you, buddy," I say, smiling the way only he can make me smile. "You're the best companion anyone could ask for."

I move into the living room, head straight to the wine rack, and pick out a bottle for dinner—my little ritual I keep to myself. I always go for red. It's not just about the drink; it's about the tradition. The pop of the cork signals that the evening can finally start on my own terms.

Dinner is simple, almost on autopilot. A plate of pasta, something quick to help my mind unwind. Toby's paws pad softly around me, his quiet presence soothing as always. He falls into step with my rhythm, and I'm more grateful for that than I ever admit.

At the table, I pour the wine and give it a moment to breathe. Sometimes I think it needs a little time, just like I do.

I lift the glass and inhale: wood, red fruit, a faint sweetness tinged with nostalgia. The first sip is warm and full, velvety on my tongue. For a moment, it eases the restlessness that hums inside me.

The pasta delivers its own sense of comfort—garlic browned in olive oil, fresh tomato, basil. I twirl a forkful. The noodles are perfectly al dente, with just enough sauce to cling to them. It's a simple, everyday flavor—but tonight, it feels especially comforting.

Toby sits beside me, eyes fixed on my plate, head tilted as if he knows exactly how to persuade me. I smile, briefly tempted, but shake my head. He yields with quiet dignity, which makes me laugh. It's almost as if he understands every thought I have.

I eat slowly, my mind wandering. Whether from fatigue or the wine, the memories slip in too easily tonight.

She comes to my mind with a clarity that both startles and hurts me. I remember her gaze—tender and involved at once. Our conversations stay with me, long and deep, briefly helping me forget the feeling of difference I've always felt. She made me believe, if only for a moment, that I could belong completely to someone—to her. It was effortless, natural, a feeling I had never known before.

But then I remember the end. Her face, drawn and tired, heavy with disappointment. The anger she felt for me for never being fully present. That was when we both understood: love wasn't enough. I still wonder if I could have done more, found a way to express myself better, been more… normal. A knot forms in my throat, a detestable sensation I know too well.

I take a long sip of wine, hoping it will lessen the weight of that memory. Tonight, it doesn't. Tonight, it cuts deeper than usual. I'm not ready to face it. Perhaps I never will be.

I leave the plate half-finished, my appetite gone, frustration creeping in. I slide the rest of the pasta to Toby, more to distract myself than to share. He wags his tail, delighted with this small victory, oblivious to the storm inside me.

I finish the last sip of wine and stare at the empty glass. Work, expectations, memories—all mixed up now, more chaos than clarity. If only answers came as easily as pouring a drink. But they don't.

No matter how I try to distract myself, my mind circles back to the same place, to the memory waiting patiently whenever I let my guard down. Tonight, I don't fight it. Whether from wine or exhaustion, I let it take over, slowly seeping in, even though it hurts.

I remember those nights with her vividly. Moments so simple, so ordinary, that anyone else might have missed them —but for me, they were the most precious part of the day.

While I cooked, she sat at the kitchen counter, watching me with that perfect mix of curiosity and amusement. She often laughed when she saw me concentrating on something particularly complicated, probably wondering if I'd succeed in pulling off whatever I was making.

"Are you sure you know what you're doing, Matt?" she'd ask with a mischievous smile, pretending to doubt my skills even though we both knew the result would be delicious. Cooking has always been one of the few things I can fully give myself to, as if it were second nature. She knew this well, but still enjoyed watching me feign concern.

"Trust me," I would reply with mock seriousness as I dramatically stirred some sauce or chopped vegetables, milking the moment for comedy. Her laughter would echo through the kitchen, filling it with warmth. Each time I glanced at her, something in me loosened, as if in those moments I was finally allowed to be myself.

When the meal was ready, I would place the plate in front of her with a nervous mix of anticipation and pride. She always stretched out the moment—waiting a few extra seconds before tasting, holding my gaze as if the suspense were part of the ritual. And then, inevitably, she would smile and say the words that dissolved my doubts:

"I always love everything you cook," she'd say with a sincere conviction that only love can give.

They were more than just meals. They were small rituals, private sanctuaries where only we existed. With her, I could laugh at nothing and forget the weight of everything else. With her, life felt bright and simple.

Why couldn't those moments last? Why couldn't I find a way to make her feel secure with me, to show how important she was, how much I loved her?

Now I sit alone, with the empty glass in front of me and silence filling the house. I would give anything to relive one of those nights again. I know it's impossible, and that truth hurts more than I want to admit.

Suddenly, Toby places his paws on my leg, pulling me back. Somehow, he always knows when to do that—when the nostalgia is about to overwhelm me.

"I'm fine, Toby," I say, though I don't quite believe it. "Thanks for being here, for always understanding."

Tonight, as on many nights before, he reminds me that there are things I still need to face and accept. Right now, it hurts too much.

"Maybe tomorrow," I whisper, as if the promise is enough to soothe my mind. I know it probably can't.

The notebook sits untouched on the nightstand. I have opened it, but the pages mostly remain blank. Someday I will fill them for real.

I don't know when, maybe tomorrow. For now, Toby is my only answer.

Humberto M. Sotomayor

2 Pending Breakfast

*"Perfect friendship
is the friendship of men
who are good, and alike in virtue, for these
wish well alike to each other qua good."*
— **Aristotle, *Nicomachean Ethics***

Seated in front of the screens that cover my workspace, my hand rests gently on the mouse. The cursor blinks slowly and persistently over the rendering of the new lobby of the corporate building. Every detail that demands my attention is there: the natural light streaming through the large windows, the carefully selected textures, the open spaces designed to convey the authentic essence of Divergent Holdings.

I take a deep breath and try to focus my attention on just one thing—perhaps the lighting or the materials. But slowly, my thoughts begin to wander, slipping away from the path I try to set for them.

My gaze stays on the wood texture I've chosen for the lobby walls. I like the warmth it adds. I wonder if I should ask for a physical sample of the material. Did I already do that? A nagging uncertainty remains, quiet but persistent, refusing to go away.

I glance away from the screen, my eyes landing on the cluttered corner of my desk: scattered notes, half-finished sketches, a pen without its cap. The thought of organizing it all flits through my mind, but I quickly realize it would just be another way to avoid the design project at hand.

I force myself once more to focus, fixing my eyes back on the main monitor. But the soft murmur of the air conditioner becomes more noticeable, and I suddenly wonder – has it always been this loud, or is it just my heightened awareness today? I make a mental note to have it checked, though it's probably just my imagination playing tricks on me.

My thoughts slip away on their own, leaving the design behind to wander through trivial details. I stare at the screen, eyes half-closed, trying to still the gentle, incessant inner murmur no one else can hear—always there, like a faint melody without end.

As I turn my chair toward the window, the world outside appears to move with calm indifference to the internal turmoil that is always present within me. Sunlight softly reflects off the building across from my office, casting brief, almost hypnotic flashes. I watch the scene quietly, letting my mind drift for a moment into those everyday flashes of light.

I turn my attention back to the main monitor, attempting once more to settle on some detail of the design, no matter how small. Then another thought surfaces with sudden clarity: maybe I shouldn't be here right now. Perhaps the day should have unfolded differently. A sense of something forgotten lingers, important, but I can't yet define what it is.

I lean back in my chair and release a slow, long sigh. My eyes drift shut as I cradle my head in my hands, trying to calm the turmoil brewing inside me. Exhaustion clings to me, a heavy weight I've somehow accumulated despite making almost no progress on the project. For a brief moment, I hold still, breathing deeply as the hush of the office settles over me.

I imagine myself walking through the lobby I am designing, moving gracefully across the spacious, luminous area. As I raise my gaze, I see natural light filtering through the tall windows, creating delicate, elegant patterns on the floor and walls. The columns I selected cast geometric shadows, shaping a calming atmosphere. The fresh, bright colors I chose align perfectly with my vision—restful and harmonious, inviting everyone to slow down and appreciate the space.

I envision the entire building as a serene refuge —a haven from the relentless pace of life, where people can breathe easily, free from the constant pressure to hurry or chase deadlines. As I linger on this mental image, I also imagine the sounds in the lobby. I want to ensure that no jarring noises intrude. It's not complete silence I'm after, but a tranquil atmosphere filled with sounds that bring calm rather than disrupt.

Suddenly, something clicks in my mind: water. That is what's missing. I can hear a gentle, natural sound—the soothing murmur of water flowing—alongside abundant greenery that brings freshness and life to the space. I vividly picture those vast, elegant gardens I have seen in luxury hotels, where water and vegetation come together to create an atmosphere of complete tranquility.

A faint smile brushes my lips at the thought, and in that instant, I'm struck by how deeply I miss traveling. It's been far too long since I've wandered, and I recall precisely why it was once a passion of mine: slipping free from routine, uncovering new landscapes, watching strangers and the subtle ways they inhabit every corner of the world. Those tiny details that might seem inconsequential to others are, to me, endlessly captivating. I cherish sitting quietly in some unfamiliar corner, simply observing, absorbing the rhythms, and uncovering something new.

Wait —the building, the lobby. My mind swiftly returns to the present, gently tugging me back from my travel daydream. Despite the detour, I feel a quiet sense of satisfaction knowing I've finally pinpointed what the design was lacking. Now, I need to determine how to infuse that element into the lobby, crafting a sense of calm without letting it dominate the space. Nothing should overshadow the rest; the lobby must remain a balanced, perfectly harmonious whole.

I attempt to brush aside the lingering unease that persists at the edge of my thoughts. Unable to identify the source, I refocus on the project, opening a new tab on my secondary monitor to search for visual references that incorporate water and greenery into interior spaces. The screen gradually fills with images of lush vertical gardens, minimalist fountains, and subtle reflecting pools.

My focus sharpens, and I feel a growing sense of confidence as I save select images to a newly created folder. I study a handful of photographs that capture the perfect balance I'm striving for: natural elements, indirect light, and soft textures that evoke the precise sense of calm I envision for the building. The concept starts to take a clear shape in my mind.

My gaze remains fixed on the screen, but my unease grows, a slow-burning tension that refuses to dissipate. I try to persuade myself that I'm making progress, but the truth is, I'm stuck in a maddening loop. Every attempt to focus only leads me down another tangent, my mind stubbornly refusing to settle. A familiar frustration begins to simmer, rising from the depths of my chest like a slow tide. I loathe these moments, this sense of being at the mercy of my own unruly thoughts.

Just as I'm about to push back from the desk, defeated by the futility of it all, my phone vibrates, its gentle buzz a minor distraction. I glance at it with a mixture of curiosity and detachment, but as I unlock the screen, a blow of reality strikes me at once: the name on it is Dave.

> "I would have preferred to have breakfast with you as we planned, Matt, but the meal was wonderful even though I had it alone. The good thing is I'm already getting used to making reservations for one."

I freeze for a few seconds, reading the message over and over, hoping it will change somehow. An uncomfortable knot tightens in my throat. Of course—that was what I had forgotten. How could I have missed breakfast with Dave? He is perhaps the only person patient enough to endure my constant distractions.

I let out a deep sigh, feeling an uneasy mix of guilt and frustration. My fingers move quickly across the screen as I attempt to craft a response that sounds sincere, though I am well aware that Dave likely expected my forgetfulness from the moment we made our plans.

I start typing a hasty reply to Dave, aiming for a casual apology that downplays my forgetfulness. But I stop almost immediately—it rings false. I delete the message and try again, this time opting for a more sincere tone, owning up to the mistake and attempting to explain. Yet, this version doesn't sit well with me either; it sounds overly formal, even defensive.

I delete the message again, as frustration simmers just below the surface. What can I say to him? How can I explain something I don't even grasp myself? My thoughts begin to tangle, racing in disjointed circles as the cursor continues to blink steadily on the screen, awaiting a response that refuses to materialize.

I toy with possible excuses, brief explanations, and even jokes that might diffuse the situation, but none of them feel authentic. I try to reconstruct my morning, wondering what led me to forget something so important. I distinctly remembered our plans the night before—so what happened? I recall waking up late, making breakfast in a hurry, and rushing out the door. Usually, when I'm meeting someone for breakfast, I leave on an empty stomach – it's a habit I'm well aware of. How did I let it slip my mind so readily?

Finally I set the phone down, unable to craft a response. I sit frozen in my chair, my gaze drifting into the void as guilt slowly takes hold – a heavy, oppressive feeling. This isn't the first time I've forgotten something important with Dave, and it likely won't be the last. I find myself wondering, not for the first time, how he continues to tolerate my recurring lapses.

Just then, the door to my office swings open, and Allison strides in, her purposeful steps faltering as she takes in my expression. She stops abruptly, her brow furrowing slightly as she tilts her head, concern etched on her face. For a brief moment, her eyes linger on mine with plain empathy, as if my distress genuinely troubles her.

"What's wrong, Matt?" she asks with concern, stepping slowly toward the desk. "I know that look all too well."

I glance at her in silence for a moment, feeling a twinge of shame.

"I forgot breakfast with Dave again," I finally admit in a low voice, my eyes shifting to the dark screen of my phone. "I don't know how he manages to put up with me, Allison. Anyone else would have given up by now."

Allison's sigh is soft, but her eyes convey a deep understanding and warmth.

"All you can do now is respond and apologize," she says firmly yet gently. "Dave knows you, Matt—he knows it's not intentional. But you need to own up to it and make amends."

I nod slowly, still uncomfortable with myself.

"Next time you make plans like that, at least let me know," Allison suggests with a gentle smile. "Maybe I can help you remember."

My gaze drifts back to the phone, still feeling that uneasy weight in my chest. Allison keeps watching me closely, waiting patiently for me to do what I know perfectly well I must. With another sigh, I finally decide to face the inevitable reply.

"You're right, Alli. I'll answer him," I tell her, attempting to inject a sense of resolve into my voice.

With a gentle nod and an approving smile, Allison leaves the office, leaving me alone with my phone and the weight of my guilt.

I pick up the phone, taking a deep breath, and reread Dave's message. Beneath his subtle humor, I detect a hint of disappointment he's trying to mask. Carefully, I begin to type again, this time with a focus on sincerity, aiming only to be honest.

> "Dave, I'm really sorry. I'm not even going to try to justify myself. You know how I am, and I know it's frustrating. Let me make it up to you soon. How about dinner this week? I promise to set three alarms this time."

I read it over several times, hesitating, but ultimately decided to send it before self-doubt crept in. The message is marked as read almost instantly. My pulse quickens slightly as I wait anxiously for his response.

After a few seconds that feel eternal, the phone finally buzzes. Dave answers swiftly, as if he had been waiting closely for my response.

"Deal, Matt. How about dinner at the house instead? Sarah would be cooking, and the kids would love to see you".

A gentle smile creeps onto my lips, and a sense of relief washes over me – faint, yet genuine. Dave has a way of reframing my mistakes, transforming them into something lighter, more approachable. I set the phone aside and lean back in my chair, feeling calm gradually seep back into my mind.

The night I met Dave was at my favorite restaurant, a hidden gem downtown where I'd often escape to disconnect from the world and find some peace. It was one of those understated yet elegant spots—a calm oasis amid the city's relentless noise.

I adore the atmosphere there, with its warm, golden lights casting a soft glow on the walls, clad in a perfect blend of exposed brick and polished dark wood. The spacious tables, dressed in crisp white linen, each feature a small lamp that creates an intimate circle of light—just enough to dine comfortably, feeling nestled in your own private space.

I always claim my spot at the bar, in the same seat, all the way to the right, near the wall. That corner allows me to see the whole room without feeling exposed, while still providing easy access to the exit—a quirk I've had for as long as I can remember.

The bar itself is a masterpiece of elegance, its surface a slab of dark marble polished to perfection. When my mind swirls with uncontrollable thoughts, I often find solace in sliding my fingertips across its cool surface, tracing imaginary patterns as though that simple gesture might help me slow the chaos inside.

James, the bartender, knows me well enough by now not to

ask too many questions. He always greets me with a brief nod, as if he understands perfectly that I come here seeking a refuge of silence and calm. Without needing to ask, he brings the wine poured with precision into a delicate, wide-bowled glass.

The same is true of my usual dinner: a bone-in New York strip, cooked medium, seared perfectly on the outside and holding that gentle blush of pink within that I always look for. Every element of the dish—from its faintly smoky aroma to its tender, juicy texture—creates an experience that's both comforting and expertly balanced.

On those nights when I dine alone, my mind wanders calmly, drifting slowly between thoughts and memories. I discreetly observe the people who usually fill the restaurant: couples conversing in hushed tones, solitary executives absorbed in the glow of their phones, the occasional family celebrating a special event, their voices reduced to a pleasant murmur that blends seamlessly with the restaurant's tranquil atmosphere.

As I wait for my meal, I often lose myself in subtler details: the soft music in the background—usually jazz or an instrumental classic that lends serenity to the space—or the delicate clink of cutlery and glasses. I like to close my eyes briefly, letting the blend of sounds wash over me—ordinary yet uniquely calming, like an auditory sanctuary that momentarily shields me from the world's chaos.

That particular night stands out in my memory; the restaurant was unusually empty, with only two other tables occupied besides mine, which added to the warm, intimate atmosphere. Absorbed in my thoughts, I watched absently as James moved behind the bar with fluid precision, calmly polishing a glass, when I heard the door open softly, announcing a newcomer.

At first, I don't pay much attention, as I always keep a certain distance from whoever walks in. But I sense someone moving slowly toward the bar, stopping just beside the empty seat next to me. When I glance over, I notice it's someone I haven't seen before: tall, with a relaxed posture, slightly tousled hair, and a natural, genuine smile. His eyes pause curiously on every detail of the room, as if he were truly absorbing the space around him.

He studied the empty seat beside me with exaggerated interest, then turned to me with a comically concerned look – clearly false, yet endearing.

"This place is packed tonight," he said with a playful tone, gesturing to the sea of empty chairs around us. "Would you mind terribly if I sat here?"

I straightened my back instinctively, my fingers tightening around the marble as if I needed its cool surface to anchor myself. My initial instinct was to pull back, to keep my distance – a habitual reflex before I allowed myself to open up.

I studied him for a few seconds, surprised, yet unable to hold back a faint smile at the absurdity—and the charm—of his remark. Usually, the thought of sharing my space with a stranger would have triggered anxiety, discomfort, and a hint of wariness. However, there was something about his spontaneous and genuine approach that made me feel unexpectedly at ease.

"I suppose you could sit," I finally replied, trying to sound indifferent, though my smile had already betrayed any attempt at distance. "Just try not to make me too uncomfortable."

He laughed softly as he took the seat beside me, carrying himself with a relaxed confidence, as if we were old friends meeting again after a long time.

"I'll do my best not to ruin your night," he said, still wearing that genuine, kind smile. "By the way, I'm Dave."

He extended his hand to me with such natural ease that I found myself taking it without hesitation, momentarily forgetting the strangeness of the situation. As our palms touched, I felt the warmth and firmness of his grip and was struck by the simple comfort of this human gesture.

"Matt," I replied simply, sensing—for some reason I could not yet explain—that the night had just taken an unexpected turn.

James approached with his usual discretion, a flicker of surprise crossing his face as he took in the scene—the eternal loner of the place—chatting easily with someone new. Dave followed James's movement, glanced at my wine glass, and nodded toward it, addressing the bartender.

"I'll have the same, please," he said with a smile both simple and assured.

James gave a slight nod and, as he stepped away to pour the wine, Dave turned back to me with a look of mild curiosity.

"Do you always come here alone?" he asked naturally, resting his arms lightly on the bar. "It seems like the kind of place you come to disconnect from the world."

I stared at him for a moment, surprised at the accuracy with which he had defined my routine. How strange that someone I had just met could so effortlessly glimpse something so essential about me.

"That's right," I replied, lifting my shoulders in a slight shrug. "There's something special about this place...I feel at peace here."

Dave nodded thoughtfully, his gaze drifting around the nearly empty room, as though he were trying to grasp the spirit of the place.

"I understand completely," he answered softly, turning his eyes back to me. "It's curious how certain places can make us feel like we belong, isn't it?"

Those simple words, spoken with utter sincerity, resonated more deeply than I expected. "To belong" was a phrase I'd rarely uttered, precisely because it was a feeling I'd experienced so in-

frequently in my life. Yet Dave spoke of it with disarming ease, as if it were the most ordinary, everyday thing.

"Yes, I think you're right," I replied with a faint smile, turning my gaze slightly away, feeling how the conversation was slowly crossing that invisible barrier I usually kept between myself and others.

At that moment, James returned with Dave's glass, setting it discreetly on the bar before withdrawing again, leaving us alone. Dave lifted his glass lightly in my direction, a gesture casual yet genuine.

"Then let's toast to those few places that make us feel that way," he said with a warm smile.

We gently clinked glasses, and as I took a sip of the wine, I felt that—for the first time in a long while—sharing my space with someone did not feel so strange. On the contrary, it felt surprisingly good.

As the night wore on, I found myself increasingly surprised by how effortlessly I could talk with Dave. Usually, after a few superficial exchanges, I'd lose interest or grow restless, searching for an excuse to leave early. But with Dave, something different happened. There was a natural spontaneity in him, something genuine that made it impossible not to pay attention.

We talked for hours about everyday things—from our culinary tastes to the books that had shaped us. The conversation flowed effortlessly, flowing from one subject to the next, and though I initially found myself parsing every word, I soon realized it wasn't necessary.

That night, I learned a lot about him. Dave was a clinical psychologist and professor at Southern Methodist University, renowned in Dallas for its esteemed psychology program. He spoke about his work with unassuming enthusiasm, casually mentioning his research projects on mental health and interpersonal relations-

hips. The way he described his profession left no doubt about his genuine passion and commitment.

He shared a little about his personal life—something I wouldn't normally expect in a first conversation. He spoke about his wife, Sarah, with an affection that shone through in every word. He told me how they had met in university, and how the simplicity of that first exchange had quickly convinced him she was the one he wanted to spend his life with.

He spoke about his two young children, Lucas and Emma, ages six and eight, with contagious enthusiasm, describing their personalities with the precise insight of someone who knows them intimately and the unmistakable pride of a father truly present in their lives.

I was struck by the ease with which Dave shared these stories—not as an attempt to boast, but as a natural, intrinsic part of who he was. As I listened to each detail of his life, I felt a strange yet comforting connection, one I usually refuse to allow myself. Dave seemed to intuitively understand my nature, respecting my pauses and small reflective silences without discomfort, giving me space while remaining warmly and steadily present.

Perhaps what ultimately made that night the start of a friendship was precisely this: Dave never tried to change me, nor did my differences seem to faze him. On the contrary, he seemed to genuinely enjoy the conversation just as it was, without expectations or judgment.

When we finally said goodbye that night, exchanging phone numbers almost instinctively, I was surprised by how much the prospect of speaking with him again lifted my spirits. As I walked to my car under the deep stillness of the night, I felt a palpable sense that something significant had shifted. Dave had somehow managed to open a door in my life that I hadn't even realized was closed.

41

Now, sitting in my office with the phone still in my hand and Dave's reply on the screen, I smile softly as I remember that first night. It's remarkable how certain unexpected encounters can shift the trajectory of your life, offering you something you never knew you needed.

Of course, our friendship hasn't been immune to my forgetfulness, absentmindedness, and the small mistakes that seem inherent to my nature. But Dave has always managed to simplify the complicated and soften the impact of my missteps, making them feel less consequential than I'd imagined.

I glance at the conversation on the screen again, feeling a deep sense of gratitude for having someone like him in my life. Our friendship came without seeking, yet it turned out to be deeply precious.

Since then, though gradually, I've felt Dave's steady, patient presence begin to shift my self-perception, ever so slightly. It's not a dramatic or sudden change; instead, it's a subtle feeling, almost imperceptible. Perhaps, in the end, I don't need to fully grasp why Dave finds it so easy to understand me. Maybe it's enough simply to accept that he does, and that for some mysterious reason, he genuinely seems to enjoy my company.

A light knock at the door gently pulls me out of my reflection.

"Matt, do you have a moment?" Samuel asks with a nervous smile. "I wanted to go over a few details with you."

I nod calmly, put my phone away, and turn in my chair to face him.

"Of course, come in, Samuel. Actually, I wanted to discuss something with you, too," I say, gesturing to the seat across from my desk.

He comes in slowly and sits with that composure he always shows, though I know he's usually far less relaxed inside than he appears.

"Something happened with the design?" he asks, with a hint of unease in his voice. "I thought we'd made good progress the other day."

"Don't worry, it's something good," I tell him with a steady smile, trying to ease his anxiety. "I've been thinking about the lobby. I think I've found exactly what it was missing. I want to add some elements of water and greenery, to create a more relaxed, more harmonious atmosphere—something that truly invites people to slow down when they enter our building."

Samuel's gaze lingers on mine, and he nods thoughtfully as his expression shifts from initial concern to genuine interest.

"That sounds great, Matt," he says finally, clearly enthusiastic. "I think it could really make an impact. Do you have any visuals to share?"

"Yes, I've been searching for references all morning," I reply, turning the secondary monitor toward him to display the images I saved earlier. "Look—here are some ideas for vertical gardens, minimalist fountains, and reflecting pools. I'm thinking of something understated that brings a sense of calm without overpowering the space."

Samuel studies each image closely, leaning slightly toward the monitor as he analyzes every detail with his characteristic precision.

"I like this idea," he says at last, pointing to one in particular that shows a discreet fountain set among greenery. "I think it would fit perfectly with what we want to convey. It's elegant, subtle, but it brings exactly the tranquility you mentioned."

A wave of relief and excitement settles in my chest at hearing his approval.

"Exactly what I was thinking," I reply with a sincere smile. "Do you think we can develop something like this with the team?"

Samuel nods quickly, his emotions now showing more openly.

"Absolutely, Matt," he says with conviction. "I'd love to start working on this. I think it could be the exact touch that sets our project apart," he says, his enthusiasm clear. "Would you like me to prepare some proposals for tomorrow?"

"That would be perfect," I reply, feeling a renewed sense of calm as the ideas begin to take shape. "I knew I could count on you to bring this to life."

"Thank you for trusting me with this, Matt," he says sincerely. "I truly believe we can create something remarkable here."

"I'm sure of it," I reply with a gentle smile, satisfied with the direction the project is taking. "Now tell me, Samuel, what was it you wanted to discuss with me earlier? You said you had a few details pending."

Samuel pauses at the door, suddenly remembering the original reason he'd come to my office. He returns to the chair and opens the folder he'd left on the table, pulling out documents and technical plans that he spreads carefully across my desk.

"Yes, I almost forgot," he says, slightly embarrassed, though he quickly regains his usual focus. "We need to decide on the final material for the lobby panels. I requested several physical samples to review, but two options stand out to me. Both fit our vision, but I'd love your input before making a final decision."

I lean forward, intrigued, and study the plans Samuel has laid out. My doubts and distractions momentarily forgotten, I focus on the task at hand.

My thoughts finally anchor to something concrete, and for several minutes, we lose ourselves in the technical details, deciding together on the necessary adjustments.

I may not have solved it all, but Samuel will walk away feeling satisfied—and some days, even a little progress feels like a small victory.

Humberto M. Sotomayor

3 Almost Successful

The conference room holds its breath, waiting for the start. It is not full yet; people keep arriving. The air feels heavy with the collective weight of expectation, as if each attendee is leaving behind a lingering thread of anxiety. Disjointed voices murmur in the background, a fragile tapestry of unfinished thoughts, interrupted laughter, and the soft scratch of notebooks against fabric. Scents gather in layers—the richness of freshly brewed coffee, the acrid tang of overheated cables, and the cloying sweetness of perfume masquerading as luxury. The stage lights hang in place, steady as expectant arrows holding back their strike.

In the improvised dressing room, time stands still. Footsteps and echoes fade into the background, replaced by the sound of my own held breath. The Ritalin pill lingers between my fingers, a moment of hesitation stretching into an eternity. I've never seen it as a miracle cure, just a fragile lifeline that keeps me grounded. I see it like a taut thread holding me precariously to the edge of sanity, a reminder that I can stand firm amid the chaos without losing my footing. As I slip it under my tongue, a private, awkward question surfaces: would I be the same person without this small chemical help?

My hands are slick with sweat, and I discreetly wipe them on my trousers. My jaw is clenched, shoulders stiff, as if burdened by an unseen weight. The projector remote in my pocket feels cool and metallic, a small object transformed into a talisman by my nervous grip. For the third time, I mentally rehearse the presentation, though I know it's not my memory that's the problem – it's doubt, the fissure that insists on opening up just before every crucial moment.

Beyond the door, the murmur of voices rises and falls like a tide. A single minute feels like an eternity. I breathe in, and then breathe out again—my heart pounds in my chest, as if trying to forge its own frantic rhythm.

The door swings open, and the murmur of the room washes over me like a wave. I step into the side aisle, feeling like I'm crossing an invisible bridge, each step carrying me closer to a point of no return. The stage looms before me, a threshold that separates anonymity from exposure. The light settles on my forehead, its warmth almost palpable, as if searing the start of the ritual into my skin.

The remote in my hand feels suddenly weighted, as if the entire outcome hinges on this small, unassuming device. My fingers tighten around it, the metal edge biting into my skin. I breathe. I take one more breath before a voice – my own – is called upon.

"Good afternoon," I say, startled by the sound: deep, steady, as if it belonged to someone else, more confident.

The silence in the room shifts, expectant.

"This project was born from a simple question," I continue. "How can we build a space that doesn't just shelter people, but invites them to feel part of it? We are not speaking only of walls or ceilings, but of a place that greets you with open arms."

I pause, letting the words settle. Some lean forward, attentive.

"This building, soon to be the new home of our company, was meant to be more than walls and offices. It had to be an example of what we want our designs to convey. Not just a workplace, but a place that embodies what we believe."

"What you will see today is not merely a building. It is an attempt at an answer. A search for belonging translated into spaces, textures, and sensations."

I press the remote, and the first image flickers to life on the screen: the building's façade. Clean lines. Glass that seems to capture the light, as if anticipating the inevitable darkness. Volumes that breathe, blending seamlessly into the cityscape.

I speak, my words unfolding not with the urgency of a technician defending a plan, but with the tenderness of someone sharing something personal. The ground floor, I explain, isn't a barrier but an open space that invites calm. The lobby isn't a loud introduction, but a gentle pause that welcomes you in. The materials, too, stay true to themselves: stone bearing its own history, wood flagrantly wood, water not ornamentation but lifeblood.

As I speak, I feel the room's atmosphere subtly shift. The audience's attention deepens. Heads nod, pens hover, as they resume their notes. The screen's glow illuminates my face, but it's as if my inner vision is being projected outward. Each sentence reaches for a place where connection and belonging might take hold. Though my words describe a building, I know I'm revealing something far more personal – myself.

A hand rises in the third row with a deliberate and precise gesture. I recognize the face: thick-rimmed glasses, a leather notebook, the gaze of someone who writes not to understand but to dissect.

"How do you make sure aesthetics do not overshadow function?" he asks. His tone seems neutral, yet his eyes search for cracks.

The silence in the room sharpens into a single point. I swallow, the remote in my hand feeling like a talisman. I take a breath before answering—not in haste, but with the care of someone walking on thin ice.

"By making them the same thing," I say, my voice steady, "natural light isn't just a whim—it reduces energy consumption and guides orientation. The columns are positioned where the structure requires them, but they don't cast harsh shadows across the walkways. Water helps regulate sound, softening the frequencies that can overwhelm the ear during peak hours. The materials used are not merely decorative; they are durable, age gracefully, and carry the story of their use."

A few nods. The journalist writes without lifting his eyes. I take it as a point in my favor, though my mind keeps wondering whether he noted the answer or the doubt.

Another hand raises two rows back. A young man, with a rumpled shirt and a quicker voice, asks:

"What makes this project different from other corporate buildings?"

The question cuts, but it also presents an opportunity. I allow myself the faintest smile.

"Perhaps the difference lies in how we see offices – not as mere containers for people, but as spaces that slow the heartbeat of those who live within them. We don't design to occupy space; we design to foster belonging."

The words linger in the air. A woman in the first row nods slowly, granting me a breath of relief—a micro-victory.

The questions keep coming—one about costs, another about deadlines—and I respond with a calm confidence developed through extensive preparation. Each answer is clear, and with every response, I sense the ground beneath me becoming firmer, as the uncertainty melts away, giving way to solid footing.

Yet, beneath that newfound confidence, another voice resonates: don't sound rehearsed, don't sound arrogant, don't sound hollow. I contain it, gripping it tightly like fragile glass that might shatter if I let go.

Then, a hand rises from the back. He stands up, his voice deep and assured—the kind that reflects years of experience in interviews.

"Don't you worry that emphasizing sensory experience could make the building a luxury instead of a necessity?"

The question struck like a sharp blow, slicing through the room like a dart, its impact lingering long after. Heads turned toward me, waiting for a crack to appear.

I take a deep breath. The inner voice whispers: answer slowly, don't rush, and don't justify more than necessary.

"True luxury," I say, choosing my words carefully, "is not found in marble lobbies, but in spaces that encourage people to slow down and feel less isolated in their daily routines. If that is what we call luxury, then I believe the world could use more of it."

A brief silence follows, then the sound of pens on paper. I notice a few restrained smiles. The ice beneath my feet feels more like solid ground.

I reach the final slide without stumbling. A moment of silence follows—and then it happens: applause, timid at first, like distant rain, swelling into a tide that covers everything.

The sound is more than mere noise; it surges through my chest, shakes my ribs, and presses inward. Each clap is a heartbeat not my own, yet one that suddenly supports me.

The room bursts into a wave of reactions. Some people nod with bright smiles, while others lean forward, as if they had been waiting for this moment. I notice two journalists standing up, their figures illuminated by the projector's light, resembling a photograph of someone else. It feels as if I am not the main character in this scene, but rather a stranger stepping into a role I was always meant to play.

The applause grows, enveloping me in a captivating wave that is almost hypnotic. It washes over me like a slow-motion revelation, as if trying to engrave the word "success" into my very essence. The heat of the spotlights mingles with the warmth of the audience, and for a moment, everything feels perfectly aligned—the project, the people, and me.

Just when it seems the celebration will not be interrupted, I feel the first tug of the rope. A tingling sensation runs through my neck, and my muscles tighten against my will. Though my smile remains fixed, another voice inside me begins to chatter: *Did I express that well enough? Did my comments about making the same decision come off as arrogant? Why did I hesitate for half a second on slide four?*

The body craves celebration, while the mind seeks examination.

I step down from the platform, the heat of the lights still clinging to my skin. Samuel grabs my forearm; his brief, firm grip pulls me back to the present moment.

"Brutal, Matt," he says, and for the first time in weeks, his jaw finally relaxes. Allison is silent; her swift, tight hug speaks volumes. She slips a bottle of water into my hand, steadying me like an anchor.

I scrawl two signatures, exchange a few smiles in the hallway, and promise to send a dossier. Then I head toward the parking lot, the applause still echoing in my mind. Suddenly, without warning, everything shifts. The reel begins to spin backward with relentless precision—my chest tightens. My breath catches. The air isn't cold, yet my hands feel icy.

The parking lot carries the smell of wet concrete and old gasoline. Every step feels empty, as if the applause has been shut away, confined behind the walls of the hall. The echoes of the applause still trail behind me, clinging to my heels, but they no longer celebrate. Instead, they drift like a distant hum, blending with the rhythm of my own breath.

I drive in silence, watching the streetlights slip by like the pendulum of a tireless clock: light, shadow, light, shadow. Between the beats, my mind rewinds the tape with merciless precision: Did I linger too long on the acoustics? Did I sound proud? Why hesitate when I know my project inside and out? The steering wheel feels slick beneath my cold hands.

At the door, Toby greets me as if I were the only person in the world. His joy is unconditional and demands nothing in return. It's a language I always understand. He leaps up, his tail wagging vigorously, and his muzzle presses against my leg, carrying the steady weight of "I'm here." I run my hand over his head, and the tension within me eases—just a little, but enough to let me breathe again.

I set the bottle of water on the table and fumble with my tie, loosening it awkwardly. The kitchen is tidy—thank you, universe; thank you, Allison; thank you, Rosa. I uncork a bottle of wine, and the cork lets out a gentle sigh, the kind that usually calms me. Tonight, it only offers me partial comfort.

With a glass in hand, I walk into the living room and take a seat, resting the notebook across my lap. I open it and gaze at the blank page, which reflects me like an unyielding mirror. Perhaps if I pour my thoughts into words, I'll be able to understand them—or at least quiet the incessant whirl of ideas in my mind.

I start to write slowly and carefully, as if each word bore more weight than the paper was ever intended to hold.

"Everyone praised today's event, but as I head home, I can't shake the feeling that I've left something important behind in a drawer. The building conveys a sense of belonging, yet I still feel like a stranger in my own creation. Why is it that when everything seems to go well, my mind always finds a way to search for flaws?"

I let the pen breathe before moving on.

"I took the pill on time, and my inner voice behaved better, but it was still there—like a coach on the sidelines: now look to the left, now pause, smile without showing my teeth. The room was full, and I was busy scanning for emergency exits. I felt triumphant on stage, but I felt defeated in the hallway on my way back. Is this what it means to be an adult? To hold two conflicting truths at once without letting them clash?"

I close my eyes. The wine carries the flavor of oak—and of questions that will not fall silent.

Amarillo, Junior High dance.

The lights spin like erratic planets, casting green and violet flashes across the bare walls. The air is thick with the scents of spilled soda, harsh disinfectant, and teenagers' anxiety. Heat accumulates in the corners, blending pressed bodies, overpowering perfumes, and fresh sweat with the smoke drifting in from the entrance. *The music pounds with a familiar rhythm, yet it still struggles to resonate within me.*

I stand against the wall, clutching a plastic cup of soda. The ice clinks against the sides, like a persistent ticking. Condensation trickles down my fingers, chilling my skin and reminding me that I'm still here—still motionless. The shirt clings tightly to my shoulders, and the tag at the back of my neck scratches uncomfortably. Everything seems to conspire to remind me that I don't belong.

In front of me, groups of kids huddle close together, then suddenly disperse, forming circles that shift and reshape at will. Their talking, laughing, and dancing seem as effortless as breathing. Shoes flash under the lights, and although their steps are a bit clumsy, they create patterns that resemble something rehearsed. Laughter pierces through the music—sharp and synchronized, like a secret code I was never given.

I watch from the edge, trying to decipher their language. How do they know when to move closer? Which words to choose? Where to place their hands? Maybe it's instinct, or perhaps it's a skill passed down that I somehow missed.

Occasionally, someone darts across the gym, while another leaps into the crowd with a confidence that eludes me. Meanwhile, I stay frozen in place, clutching my cup as if it's my only lifeline.

A teacher passes by, his shadow lingering like smoke from a cigarette, wearing a crooked vest. He gives me a brief smile that carries a hint of condescension.

"Just flow, Matt," he says as he walks on, seemingly believing he has just given me the key to the universe.

Flow. A word so simple to pronounce, yet impossible for me to live. In my mind, water never runs free—it searches for dams, it pools in layers, it stiffens into angles and silences. I open my eyes. The blank page still waits in the notebook, as if asking whether I will ever learn to Flow.

I go back to the page:

> *"Today, during the presentation, they told me once more: 'Flow.' I smiled. It's not that I can't. It's that my way of flowing is different: through layers, through angles, through silences. Sometimes people mistake that for coldness. It isn't. It's care."*

I pause to breathe. The wine carries hints of leather, and I wonder if tasters create metaphors to express what eludes definition. Perhaps this writing is my interpretation of the day. I turn the page.

> *"I know the project is good. I feel it in my body: the details align, the lobby breathes, and people will find themselves less alone within those walls. Applause, the emails that will come tomorrow, the meetings yet to be set—they all call it success. I call it almost, for the outside shone flawless, while the inside kept its echo. And still... today, for a few brief minutes, I, too, belonged."*

I close the notebook gently, not with a slam, but with a gesture that says "enough for today." I set it down on the table beside the glass, like laying down a weight and letting it rest.

In the kitchen, I put water on to boil. The bubbling breaks the silence of the house. I toss in pasta without checking the time. Garlic crackles in oil, and that domestic sound grounds me. The aroma wafts slowly, genuinely. I serve a small portion and eat slowly. The world narrows to what I can name: plate, fork, cheese, breath.

Toby curls up at my feet, coiled like a secret that asks for nothing more than to exist. I exhale alongside him.

Before turning out the lights, I set three alarms on my phone: small reminders that tomorrow will be a balancing act. One alarm to call Samuel, another to check in with Allison about the deliveries, and another just to remind me to eat. Small victories against the chaos.

In the bedroom, the house leans into silence rather than darkness. Toby scratches the blanket, circles twice, then folds himself into the corner of the bed. I lie down. My mind still murmurs, but no longer cries out. It replays the day like a lesson to be learned by heart. This time, I allow it: for tonight, it may stay.

I close my eyes with a quiet certainty, no larger than a secret: the building we presented is teaching me what I am slow to understand—that belonging is not a destination, but a gesture repeated, a hidden spring that never stops running.

Toby sighs. I sigh with him. And for the first time today, it is enough.

Humberto M. Sotomayor

4 Shadows of the Past

"Love consists in this:
two solitudes that meet,
protect and greet each other."
— **Rainer Maria Rilke, *Letters to a Young Poet***

The email arrives mid-morning, just as I am about to lose myself again in the digital stone texture covering the lobby wall. The notification's chime slices through the air with the quiet precision of a small knife. It could have been Allison with a reminder, Samuel with a question about the structure, or a supplier pressing for a delivery. But the name in the subject line jolts me to attention like a sudden, sharp brake: Elena Ramírez.

My finger hovers over the phone screen, suspended in a moment of hesitation. Before opening the email, I notice subtle details around me: the drone of the air conditioning, a reflection stretching across the monitor, and the faint scent of over-brewed coffee – that familiar, overlooked smell that rises and falls with the office air. My gaze remains fixed on the rendering, taking in the diagonal strokes of light, the soft shadows, and the water feature we fine-tuned yesterday, all intended to evoke serenity. How ironic, I think. Water meant to soothe the world, while mine has just set off all its silent alarms.

I set the phone face down, as if reversing its state could undo the moment, and pull my chair closer to the desk. The pencil tip taps out a staccato rhythm on the aluminum edge: Tick, tick, tick, tick. I focus on the task list, which includes verifying the joint detail between the wooden panels and the slab, confirming acoustic coefficients, contacting the materials department, and requesting the revised calculation file from Samuel. I zoom in, zoom out, and zoom in again. The cursor blinks steadily over a dimension line, expectant, but I remain stuck, unable to deliver.

I close my eyes for a moment, the email's contents unfolding in my mind like a foregone conclusion: "Matt, I hope you're well. I'm working with Horizon Group, and our team is interested in collaborating with Divergent Holdings on the building project. Can we meet this week to discuss details? I know it's been a while, but it would be good to see you. – Elena."

I know it without reading it—or perhaps I've already read it, between the lines of all we never said. I hold my breath, then let it go.

I stand and habit guides my feet to the coffee maker—though coffee is the last thing on my mind.

The pot, half-empty, exudes the bitter scent of reheated brew. I've been reheated myself, more times than I care to count. I changed the filter with absurd concentration, fitted the filter basket, and poured the water. The drip begins like a light rain falling inside a tent. I linger, mesmerized by the sound, as nothing seems to happen, yet everything unfolds.

"All good, Matt?" Allison appears without a sound; I never know how she manages to cross the office like a cat in heels. She carries a folder, a pen, and that look that seems to know everything I never say.

"Yeah," I answer too quickly, staring down at the coffee maker.

Allison sets the folder on the counter and watches me. She waits, then leans in to sniff the coffee, her nose wrinkling in distaste.

"Second boil?"

"Third," I admit, finally meeting her gaze.

Her eyes narrow slightly, a mixture of laughter and mild reprimand.

"I brought the quotes for the low-emissivity glass and the supplier's confirmation for the wood," she says, her finger tapping the folder. "And a message from Samuel: he left the latest version of the model on the server. And..." She pauses, letting the silence speak for itself. "There's something else, isn't there?"

"Elena," I say, the name, bare and unadorned, hangs between us like a taut rope.

Allison exhales slowly, relaxing into the moment. She leans a hip against the counter, folds her arms, and waits.

"She wrote to me," I add. "Horizon. Collaboration. Meeting."

Uh-huh," she says, her tone neutral, neither surprised nor judgmental—just familiar ground.

"I haven't seen her in three years," I go on. "And I don't know if I can..."—I press a hand to my temple—"I don't know if I can be in the same room and not do... this." My hands unfold, a gesture that maps out a complex web of possibilities.

Allison nods, still unmoving.

"Did you answer her?"

"No. Not yet."

"Good," she says. "Then we still have time to keep you from going over the cliff of impulsiveness or avoidance." Her voice is gentle, yet firm.

I force a laugh, the sound lacking genuine joy.

"Thanks for the vote of confidence."

"I have a script for you," she says, opening the folder as if she'd been waiting for this moment. She pulls out a sheet of paper and sets it on the counter in front of me. "I received your email. Thank you for thinking of us. I believe it's worth exploring the collaboration. Allison can coordinate a time and date. Best regards, Matt." Professional. Concise. No emotional promises, no hidden meanings.

"I could write that," I say.

"You could," she responds, her gaze completing the unspoken thought: You could, and you'll survive. Then she adds, "If you prefer, I can send it from my email. Just to make it clear you're on board, not running away."

"I'm not sure if…" I begin.

"Matt," she interrupts gently. "You cannot be ready and still show up. Those are different things. Today, this is work. The rest… will come when it comes."

I take the sheet and reread it. "Allison can coordinate." It's a lifeline with a name, a way to participate without exposing myself. I nod, tuck the sheet into my pocket.

"Thanks, Alli."

She pats the folder.

"That's what I'm paid for," she says with an ironic smile. "And for reminding you to eat. By the way, I left a turkey wrap in the fridge. No excuses."

"Yes, mom," I respond automatically.

She smiles. Before leaving, she pauses at the door.

"Matt…" she says. I look up. "Don't let your head win this one. I've seen you win harder things."

"Such as?"

"You've beaten the idea that you don't belong," she says. "Even if only for moments. And a moment is all it takes to cross a bridge."

She leaves. The door closes silently. The coffee maker keeps dripping.

I pick up the phone, turn it over, and open the email. I read it from start to finish without breathing.

> "Matt, I hope you're doing well. I'm working with Horizon Group, and our team is interested in collaborating with Divergent Holdings on the building project. Can we meet this week to discuss details? I know it's been a while, but it would be good to see you. —Elena"

It's professional. It's measured. All my ghosts live between those two adjectives.

I type a reply. Delete it. Type another. Delete it again. I end up writing exactly Allison's phrase, with a small, almost imperceptible addition:

> "I received your email. Thank you for considering us. I believe it's worth exploring the collaboration. Allison can coordinate a time and date. I look forward to the details. —Matt"

I pause. Click Send. The world keeps spinning. The coffee maker, the air conditioning's whirr, the rendering process—all continue uninterrupted. Yet the room feels slightly altered, as if the furniture had been nudged ever so slightly.

I refocus on the screen and open the model. A peculiar shadow streaks across the lobby; it's merely a misplaced sun effect, but for an instant, I envision a figure approaching the desk, a familiar gesture, a voice that draws me out of the virtual space.

The day drifts by, the hours slipping past without ever settling. I make a few calls, sign two documents, and test the joint between the stone edge and the glass three times, ensuring it aligns to the millimeter. Samuel moves in and out with his usual quietness, but I can tell he's pleased with how we resolved the staircase. I confirm the curve's radius and the handrail's alignment. He listens, nods, and takes notes.

Allison sends me a mid-afternoon message with confirmations:

> "Thursday, 10:00 a.m., Horizon. Conference Room 3. I'll come with you."

Just reading "I'll come with you" eases the tightness at the back of my neck.

At six, I decide to leave early. It isn't early, but for me it is. I switch off the desk lamp, pick up my pencil, and log off the computer. Toby jumps down from the office couch—I like having him with me at the office when I know I won't be going anywhere else—and trots after me with that cheerful, confident dog walk.

Allison intercepts me in the hallway.

"I'll send you the summary of pending items tonight," she says. "Need anything else?"

"Just remind me tomorrow about the east-wing panels," I answer.

"It's already on your calendar. And, Matt...", she pauses, "save the rest of the evening for yourself. No emails."

"I'll try," I say.

She gives me a look. She doesn't buy that trying.

"You will," she corrects, like someone fixing a poorly drawn line on a plan.

I smile, resigned.

In the elevator, alone, the steel surface reflects a version of me that flickers with light. The ride down to the parking level is brief. The concrete exhales its cold. I get into the car. Toby hops onto the passenger seat and settles in; his collar makes a soft, discreet jingling sound.

I start the engine. The stereo kicks in with a country playlist; I let it play for a few bars before switching to soft jazz—double bass and brushes stroking the cymbals. The change is like dimming a lamp. I pull out onto the avenue: the city at this hour is a continuous ribbon of red lights, breathing in and fading out with the rhythm of traffic. I let myself drift with that pulse; for a few minutes, I think about nothing… and, at the same time, about everything.

At a stoplight, two cars ahead, a woman crosses the street with her hair tied in a low bun, a few loose strands framing her neck. She isn't Elena, but for three seconds, my body decides she is. It's incredible how quickly the mind can conjure a presence. The woman disappears into the crowd. I am left with the trace of an imagined perfume.

The light changes. I move forward. The next stop, shorter, gifts me a small memory—one that doesn't hurt for what it was but for what I failed to see.

We're standing in line at a bakery on a Saturday morning; the air smells of warm flour and freshly ground coffee. Elena tugs at my sleeve and, with a sly smile, whispers, "Get the vanilla doughnut, not the chocolate one—trust me. I'm not one to trust easily, but I

65

do. The vanilla one has that soft texture, that exact taste of a childhood that isn't mine, and it makes me laugh without knowing why. I convey it with a glance; she nods, as if she'd been expecting that gesture all along. That day, everything seemed easy. Nothing was. But for a little while, it was.

I'm back.

The horn behind me reminds me I'm a man driving home on an ordinary afternoon. I turn right. The sun falls to one side, tinting the facades with a copper hue. I think—as if wishing could change anything— I hope Thursday is warm. I face things better on warm days.

Toby trots ahead down the hallway as soon as I open the door. He rests his front paws on my thigh, burying his snout in my hand as if that alone could pull me back into the present. It works. I close the door. The house smells of clean wood and that damp stone scent that I've always liked. The living room lights glow warmly at half intensity. I drop my keys into the metal dish— its familiar sound greets me. I head to the kitchen and open the fridge. A glass container with leftover pasta—"thank you, immediate past"— awaits me alongside a bag of greens in the drawer. I take out a glass and a bottle. The cork pops out with that sigh that always makes me think someone, somewhere, invented a distinct sound for every act that soothes. I pour a small amount: it's not a night for a long glass of wine, only for a sip to keep company.

I could put on music, but I don't. I prefer letting the silence settle into the corners. I heat the pasta while watching the blue flame in its small dance. The hypnotic movement holds me for a few seconds, until my mind interrupts with a growing list: tomorrow, I need to call acoustics; on Thursday... Elena. The thought brings a faint vertigo.

I set Toby's dinner down. He sits before I even ask, eating happily with the practical enthusiasm of someone who knows how to enjoy what's in front of him. I envy him a little.

I carry my plate to the table. The wood is cool beneath my forearms; I like leaning my weight on it, as if the table could support me beyond just my posture. I take a bite—the pasta is better than it was last night; some flavors settle overnight before they find themselves. I take a small sip of wine and shut my eyes. It lingers with a hint of wood and something my mind names plum, though I'm not sure if that's a real thing. I'm not thinking about wine tastings; I'm thinking about anchors.

The phone vibrates. I ignore it. It vibrates again. I glance at it: Allison.

> "Thursday confirmed. I'll pick you up at 9:20. No discussion. Good night."

I respond with a thumbs up and set the phone face down again. Over time, that gesture has become a boundary—a way of saying, "that's enough for today."

The night calls for something other than work. I walk to the living room and sink into the couch. Toby snuggles up next to me, warm and tucked in, as if his warmth knows precisely how to fill the space I'm missing. The corner lamp casts a soft cone of light that barely grazes the carpet, outlining calm shadows.

I glance over at the bookshelf on the other side, and my eyes land on a book: "The Art of Racing in the Rain." I smile, not sure if it's a coincidence, fate, or something else.

I don't open it; I just hold it for a few seconds, lost in my own bubble, as if the weight of the book alone were enough to keep me company tonight.

I walk back slowly, carrying with me a calm I know will not last.

I turn off the dining room light, and the house folds itself into a quiet twilight. I go upstairs to my bedroom. On the nightstand, the notebook. I look at it with the caution one reserves for something that knows it'll both hurt and soothe.

Before I begin to write, my mind, as if asking permission, projects with crystal clarity the scene I've avoided so many times. The last conversation that mattered. No shouting, no fighting. Just the quiet pull of a receding tide. I'm drawn back in.

> *Friday, about three years ago. Home. Night.*
>
> *I'm cooking. I'm not sure what anymore. I remember the smell: basil, tomato, garlic simmering in oil over low heat. The knife in my hand finds a rhythm. Chopping onions always stirs something strange in me: my eyes water, but not for the reason you'd think.*
>
> *Elena is sitting at the counter, one foot bare, the other tapping the wooden stool with her toes. A book lies open in front of her, but she isn't reading. She holds it as if holding it were just enough to make the silence easier.*
>
> *"Do you remember our date yesterday?" she asks without looking up.*
>
> *My hand hesitates for a second. (Date. Yesterday.) The word "yesterday" opens a door in my head that leads to a dark room. I mentally replay my schedule: meetings in the morning, a call with the supplier, materials testing at 4, and final rendering until late. My memory flashes disjointed images—nothing about a date.*

"I forgot," I admit, setting down the knife. "I was..."

"Working," she completes, her voice without anger, just weariness. "You always are, Matt. I'm not asking you to change who you are. Just to be here. With me."

I want to tell her yes, that I was there, that it's not that I don't see her, but I was. That there is a part of me, the part that escapes into a hole when the world gets too loud, that loves her too. That I don't do it on purpose, that my mind is a labyrinth, and sometimes I lose the important things in the inner corridors, leaving crumbs that the wind sweeps away. I want to tell her that there are moments when everything is a blinding spotlight, and I don't know how to turn it off, so I shut everything down. But what I do instead is go back to the knife. I chop. I arrange. I put things in order. I sprinkle salt like someone who believes sodium heals.

Elena closes the book. Looks at me. Her eyes hold that clarity of someone who already knows. She lifts the glass of wine to her lips, doesn't take a sip. Sets it back down.

"I don't want to fight," she says. And I think: fighting would be easier.

"I'm just... telling you, I'm tired of always being the second voice in your head."

Her tone doesn't rise. It just hangs there.

I feel something physical, like the blood in my chest has hit a sudden curve. I press my hands against the marble counter—cold, smooth—and trace it as if searching for answers in the stone.

"I'm here," I say.

"You're at many places at once," she replies. "And I don't judge you for that. I love you for it, too. The way you see the world, the way you see light when it streams through a window, as if it were speaking to you. But when we're together, sometimes I need... fewer windows. Just one." She smiles sadly. "And curtains."

I close my eyes. The absurd image of a room with a single window and heavy curtains gives me a fleeting moment of grace. Then it's gone.

"I'm learning," I say. "I'm... "—I falter a little over the word—"trying."

"I know," she responds immediately. That's the worst and best thing about Elena—she knows. "And that's what hurts more. Because you try, and still..." She lets the sentence drift, as if unwilling to sign a truth she already accepts.

I serve the pasta. Set her plate in front of her, mine on the other side. We remain standing, separated by the counter. We take up our utensils as if that gesture alone could hold everything together.

"I don't want this to be a list of your flaws, Matt," she says after taking a bite. "I also..." She laughs softly. "I'm also a constellation of flaws."

"You're not," I respond automatically.

"Yes, I am," she insists without arrogance. "I get frustrated when I don't understand your silences. I assume they have to do with me, and sometimes they don't. I feel alone when you withdraw into yourself and I'm left outside, knocking on a door you don't hear. I feel small when you get lost in your world, and I become just a thread on the edge. And then I get angry at myself for feeling small. See?"

I nod. I see.

"I don't know how to be different," I say, and it's the truth that weighs the most. It's not a defense; it's a eulogy.

Elena puts down her fork and comes closer. She rests her forehead on my collarbone, and I wrap my arms around her. She smells of her usual perfume, of fresh flowers. She stays there for a moment I'd like to inhabit forever.

"I'm not asking you to be different, Matt," she whispers. "I'm

asking you to be here. And being here, for you, sometimes is... a mountain."

"I want to learn to climb it," I reply, almost in a whisper.

"I know," she says again. "And sometimes you do. And the view is beautiful. But then you get lost in the clouds." She steps back and looks at me. "I'm not leaving you today," she says with a calm that scares me. "But maybe I've been leaving for a long time. And it hurts to say it. A lot."

Her words remain suspended in the air, as if the entire kitchen had stopped to listen. I feel a void in my chest, an echo expanding until it leaves me breathless. I grip the edge of the counter, noticing the cool marble beneath my fingers, as if it could anchor me to something solid.

"I don't want to lose you," I say, with the honesty of a child who finally finds the words.

"I didn't want to lose you either," she responds. There's no reproach, just an inventory of facts.

We eat in a silence that's not punishment. It's care. We wash the dishes as if they were made of antique porcelain. The foam carries that lemon scent that erases everything, even what should have stayed. I dry a glass with a cloth that starts shedding lint. She gathers her things. She's not leaving. She sits down on the couch. I sit beside her. We don't touch.

"Can we try again?" she asks, and for a second, I hate it. The answer is yes because I love her, but I know one yes isn't enough. And no answer does justice. I just think this, and then I speak.

"We can," I say. "And we can also admit that maybe trying again is like extending a house with cracks in the columns. I speak my own language—the language of buildings. It can be reinforced. Resin can be injected. It can be propped up. But there are things that..." I trail off.

"There are things that just get left behind," she completes.

"And remembered." She looks at me with tenderness. "I'm not asking you to forget me. I'm asking you not to hurt yourself for not being what you think you should be."

The night wraps around us. She stays the night. I barely sleep. I listen to her breathe, and for the first time, the sound that had always soothed me splits something inside. The next morning, there is no fight, no slammed door. There is a long embrace at the door. A promise neither of us knows how to keep: "We'll talk."

We texted each other for a few weeks. Then life did its work as a river does. It carried us to different shores. That was the last night we spent together.

I open the notebook.

The blank page stares back at me with the transparency of an interrogation.

I run my fingertips over the paper's texture. I nod, as if we had reached some quiet agreement. I pick up the pen. I write slowly, like someone who doesn't want to wake anyone up.

"Elena messaged me today. Work stuff. Thursday at 10. I've been trying to name what I feel for hours, and the list is ridiculous: fear, relief, longing, panic, curiosity, old tenderness, guilt —both old and new—and the exact feeling of opening a door I know and yet don't.

I'm not normal. (I write it and don't know whether to laugh or to embrace the child who should have heard this said a different way.) I know my mind works like those lamps with a thousand filaments: everything lights up at once. Sometimes it's beautiful—I see what others don't, connect ideas, catch the light in things, and translate it into stone, into wood, into water. Sometimes it's a cage with too many windows—I get distracted, I lose myself, I forget appointments, I hurt people without meaning to. I wish I weren't like this. Not for me. For whoever sits next to me and has to dance to a rhythm they never chose.

With Elena, I wanted to learn a different rhythm. There were days when we managed to make it work, and we danced beautifully. There were days when the music got away from me. I wonder if seeing her now would help me close things off, and I answer that maybe it's not about closing anything that was never fully open. Perhaps it's about acknowledging that some wounds learn to live with us, transformed into scars.

I would like to tell her something on Thursday that's not another promise of change. I would like to say "thank you for living in my house when it was full of noise" and "sorry for asking you to dim the lights that were yours." I would like to ask her to enter that room with two windows: one for the work to come in, another for the past to leave, if it wants to.

I'm afraid she'll see me as before, and at the same time I want her to see me—if only for a second—with those eyes in which I used to recognize myself. Not to go back. To know that a person existed and now lives in a body, trying to make it a little more habitable.

I'm not sure if I'm ready. But I can be. I can arrive at 9:57 and take a breath before speaking. I can answer questions without needing to construct elaborate justifications. I can say, "I don't know," and also, "I can't answer that now." I can take care of that *part of me that unravels, without using it as an excuse.*

I don't want to hide.

I don't want to prove anything.

I just want to be."

I set down the pen. I am left with the phrase "I just want to be" circling like a fish in a small aquarium. Toby lifts his head, looks at me, and lets out that dog sigh that always sounds like acceptance. I pet him.

I pick up the notebook again. I add, below, as if I'm talking to her:

«*E.,*»

I won't send you this. But it feels good to write it.

"You are, still, a house in my memory—one with a kitchen and a counter where I learned to cut more than just vegetables. If we meet on Thursday, I promise not to bring any leaks. If the rain comes, I'll stand beside you so it won't drench us, but I won't try to fix the weather.

Thanks for the Saturdays of bread. Thanks for the vanilla doughnut. You taught me to trust flavors I couldn't even name.

If we're meeting to talk about work, let's keep the conversation focused on work. I'll do my part. And if the past happens to crack the door open, I'll leave it ajar—not to let it back in, but to let it breathe for a moment before it moves on."

I close the notebook, not with a slam, but as if someone were putting away a clean suit. I set it back in its usual place, feeling the weight of the paper like a warm stone on my chest.

I head to the bathroom and wash my face. The mirror, that unforgiving creature, reflects a man with slightly redder eyes and a mouth that is a little stiller. I turn off the light and go back to the kitchen. I wash the glass carefully; today, the towel leaves no lint. I put away the plate. I leave the kitchen the way I like to see it: ready to start again.

In the bedroom, the phone displays a red dot, indicating an unread email. I don't open it. I put it on silent mode. I set the alarms, the regular one and the backup, just in case. The one for being present, in case the backup one fails.

I turn off the bedside lamp. The house, in the dark, feels weightless. Toby spins around twice and curls up at my feet. I close my eyes. The image of Elena silhouetted against the noon light visits me for a second, then drifts away. Behind it, a conference room, a large table, and glasses of water remain. I can see my hands open on the wood, my fingers unmoving. I can almost hear my voice, plain and unadorned.

There's no closure today. I'm not looking for it. There's a Thursday ahead, a meeting with a name, a building that asks of us what I ask of myself: to belong without shouting, by choice, by rhythm. I tell myself —just barely—that perhaps my most serious job has never been building walls, but learning to open windows without getting lost in them.

I fall asleep with a small, modest, almost ordinary certainty: I can be in a room with Elena like an adult. Not to go back. To honor what we were by respecting what we are not anymore.

Humberto M. Sotomayor

5 Dancing Through the Noise

Thursday dawns slower than I expected. Maybe it's the insomnia, maybe it's the mental list I've been reviewing since 4:17 AM, or perhaps it's the three alarms I set to ensure I don't arrive late. Either way, the sun streams through the window, creating a tone that is both optimistic and intrusive. Toby follows me as I tidy up the kitchen and check for the third time that I have everything I need: the folder with blueprints, the iPad with the latest presentation, and a pen I like because it rolls smoothly across the page.

Allison arrives punctually at 9:20, just like she promised—and threatened—in her message. She opens the door without waiting for me to do it, as if it were her own house.

"Ready," she says, giving my outfit a quick once-over. "Good. Professional, but without looking like you're going to a wedding."

On the way, the traffic feels louder than usual. Allison talks about practical things—the pending contract with the glass supplier, the shipment of samples—but I only catch snippets. My mind keeps bouncing between two images: the rendering of the lobby and Elena's silhouette, which I haven't seen in three years.

As I arrive at Horizon Group, the lobby greets me with the scent of freshly polished wood mixed with the faint aroma of machine-brewed coffee. Light cuts across the space in perfect diagonals, as if someone had planned the exact moment we would step inside. The pale stone walls seem to absorb every sound, but I still catch the subtle echo of footsteps on the marble.

The elevator rises in near silence, broken only by the hum of its motor and by the faint glide of the cable. Allison scrolls through her tablet while I study my reflection in the stainless steel: tie straight, expression caught between composed and tense.

The conference room is set up: a long, dark-wood table, ergonomic chairs lined up with almost millimeter precision, and a large screen lit with the Horizon logo. Five glasses of water wait at each seat, their transparent surfaces catching and scattering small fragments of light.

I take my seat and, almost without thinking, start counting seconds between breaths, trying not to let my pulse set the pace. The rustle of paper and the tap of a pen on the table fill the air...

Until Elena walks in.

The click of her heels on the marble sounds different from the rest, as if the air itself recognizes her. Everyone turns to look at her.

I hadn't seen her in so long that my memory had softened some edges. Now they're back: the way she gathers her hair in an imperfect bun, the brief gesture of adjusting her watch on her wrist before sitting, the slight tilt of her head as she greets. She's just as beautiful as ever, I think, and that thought hits me with the same sharpness as the first time I saw her.

I watch her for a second longer than I should, as if I need to confirm she's real, and then I force myself to come back to the present.

The meeting is about to start, and I can't afford to lose the thread before I even say a word.

"Matt," she says, with a smile that's professional but not distant. "It's great to see you."

"Likewise," I respond, careful to keep my voice steady.

The meeting begins with formalities. One of her colleagues—a tall man with thin glasses and a pronounced Southern accent, the kind that stretches out vowels and softens consonants— starts the Horizon presentation. I focus on the slides, yet my gaze keeps drifting to the glint of water in the glasses, the projector's sheen across the polished wood of the table, and the way Elena takes notes in her right-slanted handwriting.

Then Elena takes the floor. Her tone is serene, but carries the quiet conviction that's always been there whenever she talks about a project she believes in. She explains that Horizon can contribute in two key areas: on one hand, technical support to achieve high-level sustainability certifications, integrating water harvesting systems and intelligent energy control; on the other, a more sensory layer for the lobby, fine-tuning the lighting, sound, and even the scent of the space to make the welcome experience coherent and memorable.

"We want to work with what's already there," she says. "Not to replace it. What Matt has designed already has a clear language; our job would be to refine it without distorting it."

I feel a slight knot in my stomach, as if she'd described my home without asking permission. The pen between my fingers feels suddenly weightless, and for a second, I have to set it down on the folder to keep from dropping it.

I nod, though inside I feel like someone has opened a window in a room I thought was closed. Horizon is stepping into the most personal part of my design: the water, the greenery, the calm. And it's Elena who holds the key.

She looks as perfect as ever: her straight posture, her precision in choosing words, the way her gaze sweeps the table to make sure everyone is with her.

I refocus on the slides and the voice of one of her colleagues, who takes over the technical part. The professional world demands I stay present there, but part of me keeps looking at that open window.

When it's my turn, Allison signals me with a brief look. I open my folder and begin:

"Our proposal for the lobby is based on two main elements: water and greenery. Not as decoration, but as an essential part of the experience..."

As I speak, the ground feels a bit firmer. I explain how the sound of water helps regulate the acoustics, how the plants bring visual freshness and improve air quality. The man with glasses nods. Elena looks straight at me when I mention the word "belonging," and that glance forces me to lower my eyes to the blueprint so I don't lose my train of thought.

"It's risky, but bold," Elena says when I finish. "I think that's what this project needs: a clear gesture that speaks of hospitality and calm."

I nod, not trusting my voice too much. I hold on to that word—bold—and mentally place it on a shelf.

Then comes the Q&A. One of her colleagues, younger and wearing a navy suit, asks about additional maintenance costs. I begin to answer, but Allison jumps in to clarify figures and deadlines. It's not that I don't know how to respond, but hearing her voice beside me takes some of the weight of those eyes off my shoulders.

The meeting wraps up smoothly. We set the terms for a second session and outlined the tasks to be completed. As we stand to leave, Elena steps closer.

"I'm glad to see you're still..." —her eyes linger on me for a moment—"building things that matter," she says, and there's something in her tone that's neither nostalgia nor mere courtesy.

"Thank you," I reply, and I catch myself holding her gaze for a moment longer than necessary before taking a step back.

In the hallway, while we wait for the elevator, Allison whispers to me, "You did well. You were present."

I'm not sure whether she says it to convince me or to remind me. Maybe both.

The elevator arrives. We step in and descend. Outside, the air hits me with a clarity I appreciate. I walk towards the car with the feeling that something was left hanging in the air, yet also with the relief of having crossed a bridge I had been afraid to face.

Dave's house smells like freshly fried chicken and warm cornbread, the kind of aroma that lingers in the air like an invitation. Sarah opens the door before I even ring the bell, as if she'd been standing there waiting. Her hug comes without warning, warm and complete, leaving me suspended for a second in a type of contact I don't often experience. I barely have time to react before she's already guiding me gently inside.

"Matt! I'm so glad you came," she says, and there's no hostess formality in her eyes, only the genuine brightness of someone truly happy to see you.

From the dining room, Dave raises his glass of wine. "Look who's here!" he says in that voice that fills the room. "Come on in, come on in."

I step across the threshold, and the contrast with the Horizon conference room hits me immediately—here the floor doesn't reflect the light, it absorbs it; sounds don't echo, they blend; a television in the background murmurs with low-volume cartoons. In the kitchen, the oil still sizzles softly in the pan. On the table lie scattered crayons, a tower of blocks, two glasses with colorful straws, and a book open-facedown, as if someone had left it mid-story to attend to an eight-year-old's emergency.

Sarah leads me to the dining room. "Sit wherever you like—just watch out for Lucas's LEGOs."

"They're not LEGOs," a small voice corrects from below. "It's a flying car."

I glance down, and Lucas, six, shows me a LEGO structure with improvised fins and huge wheels. "Obviously," I say, bending toward him. "A flying car. Not just anyone could build that."

At the head of the table, Emma, eight years old, is drawing on a crumpled sheet of paper. Without looking up, she hands me the paper—a dog-dragon with asymmetrical wings and a wide, beaming grin.

"For you," she says—not as an invitation, but as a decision already made.

I study the drawing carefully. It has no symmetry, no sense of proportion... and yet, there's something about it that holds me still. A kind of "chaos" that somehow feels alive.

"It's perfect," I tell her, and I'm not lying. "It looks a bit like Toby, doesn't it?"

Emma smiles, pleased. "Yes, but with powers!"

Dinner arrives in abundance at the center of the table: crispy fried chicken, mashed potatoes with thick gravy, coleslaw, and golden cornbread. Sarah serves generous portions; Dave opens another bottle of wine. The conversation jumps from one topic to another, as if everyone is dancing on a floor where the music changes without warning. I follow the rhythm as best I can—nodding, smiling, asking short questions. Between bites, I count the crayons scattered across the table, mentally lining them up by tone, which helps me when the noise starts to surround me.

Lucas invites me to help him install "the thrusters" on his flying car. I get up, and for a few minutes, the world narrows down to fitting plastic pieces together and testing improbable combinations. Lucas laughs at every suggestion I make, as if he's not used to adults playing along this much. Emma joins in, proposing that the dog-dragon pilot the vehicle. I don't question the logic; I just keep building.

"I think you're in your element," Dave says from the kitchen—half joking, half not.

And he's right. Here, I don't think about whether I should say something more, or if I'm moving "properly" at a dinner party. For moments, I let myself be carried away, as if these two little ones have found a direct access to a place where I don't need to translate myself.

After dessert—pecan pie with a scoop of vanilla ice cream—Dave raises his glass.

"To visits that are worth it," he says, looking at me in a way that I know he's not just talking about tonight.

I raise mine.

"To friends who are family."

The wine tastes fuller at this moment. Emma's laughter, the clatter of a Lego piece hitting the floor, Sarah's murmur in the kitchen... everything blends into a kind of atmosphere that's nothing like my daily life, but it feels good.

When Sarah announces it's time for the kids to sleep, Lucas and Emma protest a bit, but they eventually head upstairs amid laughter and hurried footsteps. Sarah follows them, leaving Dave and me to clear the table.

"Let me help you," I say, although I already have a plate in my hand before she responds.

Dave's kitchen is smaller than mine, but it's organized with that functional logic I always aim for and rarely manage to keep. Hot water runs over the dishes, and the steam rises in slow, spiraling movements. Dave hands me a towel to dry the dishes, and I start stacking the glasses in silence.

For a few minutes, the only sounds are the clinking of silverware against porcelain and the faint crumpling of napkins. The noise of dinner has faded away, as if the house had slowly closed its doors to the bustle.

"So... how did it go with Horizon?" Dave asks, not looking at me but with a tone that makes it clear he expects more than just 'fine.'

I dry a glass with more care than necessary.

"It went... all right. No problems."

"All right," he repeats, almost jokingly. "Translation: you didn't do anything wrong, but in your head, you've already found ten things you could have done better."

I don't laugh. I set the glass on the counter.

"Yeah. Something like that."

"And Elena?" he asks bluntly.

"She's... there," I say, leaning against the counter.

I let the silence stretch for a few seconds, until the dry knot in my throat forces me to speak.

"I loved her, Dave," I say it all at once, as if the words had been waiting for years for a crack to slip through.

The words come out faster than I expect, and as soon as I hear them floating in the air, I feel my throat tighten for a moment. Heat climbs up my neck while my hands—still cold—keep gripping the dish towel as if it were the only thing keeping me anchored to the kitchen. I feel a strange weight in my chest, as though I'd released something I'd kept sealed for too long.

Dave remains still, plate in hand. He looks at me without judgment, but with the kind of seriousness he reserves for things that matter.

"You'd never told me you loved someone," he says.

"No…" I answer. "And I suppose that's because it hadn't happened before. With her, it was different. It wasn't just… wanting to be there, it was feeling like, somehow, I could be. Like the way I am didn't scare her off. And even so… I ruined it."

Dave places a hand on my shoulder, as if to bring me back to the present.

"You ruined it?" he asks, raising an eyebrow.

"Mostly, yes. I'd get lost in my world, forget things, leave her alone even when I was right next to her. And now… seeing her, but in a conference room, talking about blueprints and certifications… It's like hearing your favorite song in a different language. You recognize the music, but there's something you can't quite reach."

Dave sets the plate down and leans against the counter beside me.

"Matt, love isn't a project you can measure by blueprints and deadlines. It doesn't work that way. And not everything that ends is broken. Sometimes it just… changes shape."

I don't reply. He continues:

"What I do know," Dave says, "is that the fact you can say 'I loved her' without hiding behind anything—that's already different. I'm telling you this because I've been there. And because maybe today's meeting wasn't just work, maybe it was proof that you can be in the same room without having everything fall apart."

The silence that follows doesn't feel heavy. We finish drying the dishes. Dave refills my glass with a bit more wine. For a moment, I feel lighter, as if the kitchen itself—the soft scent of cornbread, the warmth of the water—had washed away more than just the remains of dinner.

We slowly finish our glasses, without rushing. Sarah comes down a few minutes later, no apron now, and her hair pulled back into a loose bun. She tells us, almost in a whisper, that the kids are already asleep—Emma hugging her favorite stuffed animal, and Lucas surrounded by half of his unfinished LEGO city.

We talk a little longer about things that don't matter much: a series none of us have seen, a new restaurant we'll probably never visit, the weather that seems bent on keeping us guessing. The conversation flows on its own, like a pendulum that needs no winding.

At the door, the goodbyes stretch out with that easy cadence that only happens when you feel at home. Sarah hugs me with genuine affection; Dave gives me a pat on the back that sounds more like "we're here for you" than goodbye. The porch light casts a soft, almost cinematic glow over the entryway.

"Remember, Matt," Dave says with his usual cheerful ease, "this is your home. There will always be a place for you."

Those words linger as I walk to the car. It's not just courtesy—I can tell by the tone in his voice, as if handing me a key I'm free to use whenever I need it.

I reach my car with a strange feeling—as if I had been at home, as if, for a few hours, I had belonged to a family that wasn't mine, but who had opened a place for me at their table without conditions.

The drive back is quiet, almost no traffic. The city lights blink as if marking a path, but I don't hurry. I feel a different kind of fatigue than usual: not only in my head, but also in my body. My shoulders feel heavy, as if I'd been carrying something invisible all day; my eyelids droop more than usual, and a soft humming persists in my ears, a residual echo of all the voices, laughter, and noises that had been with me since morning. Even driving—something I can almost do with my eyes closed—feels heavier, as if every traffic light, every lane change, demanded deliberate effort.

When I park in front of the house and open the door, Toby is waiting, as always, no matter the hour or the exhaustion I'm carrying. His dark eyes seem to read me before I say a word. I crouch and run a hand along his back; the softness of his fur is a tangible reminder that here, in this house, some things don't change. He settles beside me with the precision of one who knows exactly where to be.

His breathing is slow and steady, and with each exhalation, it slows my pace a bit. He doesn't demand conversation or explanations. He's been with me through all my versions—the one that laughs without restraint, the one that withdraws into silence, the one that arrives exhausted, the one that doesn't want to talk to anyone. He never asks me to be someone else. He doesn't judge my absences or my returns; he simply stays, and in that staying, there's a kind of loyalty that can't be learned—only given.

I can't quite put it into words, but it feels like a kind of support—an "I'm here" that doesn't need to be earned. I realize that even if I can't explain the day I've had, he already knows. He perceives it in my shoulders, in my voice, in the way I drop the keys. And yet, he stays.

I sink into the couch. He rests his head on my leg, and the world narrows to that: his weight, his warmth, and the quiet certainty that, at least here, I belong. Outside, the city keeps its usual rhythm. Inside, the world has shrunk to this moment.

Everything is quiet. No music, no television, no humming of the coffee maker. Just my breathing and the soft tap of Toby's nails on the floor when he wanders through the house—either to drink water or to make sure no stranger crosses the door.

I close my eyes and let the day pass before me like a film I don't need to pause. I see the morning meeting: the words I chose, the ones I left unspoken; Elena's gaze, so direct it forced me to look away; Allison's timely intervention when my speech began to stumble. Then dinner: Lucas's unfiltered laughter, Emma's chaotic and perfect drawing, and the warmth Dave and Sarah offered unconditionally.

Everything comes back—not with the speed of analysis, but with the cadence of something that just wants to stay there, taking its place. I'm not looking for explanations or assessments.

I could take the notebook and write it all down, dissect it, look for patterns, assign blame or merit—but not tonight. Tonight, there are no doors to open in my head. Tonight, I choose not to analyze.

I tell myself, almost in a whisper, that I was present. That I showed up, I spoke, I listened. I don't know if everything went well—too little at the meeting, too much with Dave—but I want to trust that it was enough.

I get up, wash my face, and set my alarms: the usual one, the backup, and the one that reminds me to be present. Toby follows me to the bedroom and curls up at my feet, fitting his body into the exact space that seems made for him.

I turn off the light. The silence wraps around me; I don't feel the need to fill it with anything.

I fall asleep with a modest, almost fragile certainty: sometimes, the simple act of being is the real triumph.

Humberto M. Sotomayor

6 Lines of Escape

*"If you are distressed by anything external,
the pain is not due to the thing itself,
but to your estimate of it, and this
you have the power to revoke at any moment."*
— Marco Aurelio, *Meditations*

I slam my office door harder than I should. The impact bounces off the walls and settles in the glass. A drumbeat that takes a while to fade away. It doesn't calm me. I drop into the chair with the weight of an anger that feels heavier than exhaustion. The pen spins between my fingers, bumps into my thumb, slips, and the plastic cracks. I could break it; I stop myself at the last second, as if saving something so small could convince me I still have control over anything.

I breathe. I count: one, two, three, four. I slowly exhale. The whirr of the air conditioner draws a steady line, slicing the silence into two exact halves. On the screen, the VitaPlaza model remains open: a general blueprint showing the open-air corridors, the tiered patios, the folds of shadow. Green walls climb like a living breath; the reflecting pools are calm eyes that don't blink. The canopies—those quiet wings—don't announce themselves; they hide behind the greenery, ready to unfurl whenever the Texas sky decides its unpredictable mood.

"Simplify." The word drops again—clean, transactional—a coin tossed to decide something without looking. Carver pronounced it without ruffling his gray suit, drumming his fingers on the conference table in Frisco. "Fewer gardens, less water, fewer canopies. It's a mall, not a park." He said it with the certainty of someone quoting an accounting manual. Outside, behind the giant windows, the north side of the metroplex moved to the rhythm of cranes and recently laid streets; inside, Excel occupied more seats than ideas.

I relax my jaw. I realize I'd been clenching it since the meeting. Again: one, two, three, four. It doesn't work. I start counting again. I'm surprised by the tone of my own voice as it replays in my head: measured, professional, almost correct. Such a dangerous word, "correct." A room without echoes. Without music.

VitaPlaza is not a mall. I don't even think before saying it. It is—If I let myself say it the way I feel it—an open-air plaza that builds a bridge between different kinds of people: kids with dripping popsicles, grandparents searching for shade and conversation, teenagers who don't want to buy anything but need a place to belong without asking permission, couples strolling with no destination, workers taking a break with a coffee and a comfortable bench. It's a breath of air the north of Dallas didn't know it needed. It's the kind of place that creates its own language: small businesses that bloom, live music on Fridays, a weekend market, a community that recognizes itself by inhabiting the same urban gesture. If we build it right, Frisco won't just grow in square feet—it'll grow in tone.

I see it again: the vertical gardens cushioning the August heat, muffling the noise of the highway, filtering the air so the smell of food—barbecue, roasted coffee, bread rising in the oven—has room to breathe. Water, not as a luxury, but as a regulator of temperature, as a common language: the thin sheet of water that runs along a wall and sings softly; the shallow fountain where children dip their fingers; the light mist that cools the air when the sun beats down. The canopies: not that canvas that covers everything and kills the light, but canopies stretched between structures that play with the wind, that let the sky through, that ease the blow of a storm without pushing anyone inside—living shadows, not ceilings.

Carver's voice runs through my head again, that cadence I can't seem to forget: 'value engineering.' He said those two words as if he were announcing he was about to save a soul. He repeated them several times, each one more certain than the last. "Cut the super-fluous." His finger tapped against the table with a steady, relentless rhythm—like a metronome set to sixty. The rest of his team nodded; someone slid a spreadsheet across the table, full of percentages that claimed to measure everything. I tried to explain—in that tone architects use when they ask to be heard without meaning to—that the gardens aren't "decoration" but skin; that water is both acous-tics and climate; that the canopies are emotional structure and shel-ter. I spoke of belonging. That threw him off for a second. Then he went back to the numbers.

I rest my elbows on the table. The wood feels cold. I cling to that coldness. I look at the rendering and, for a moment, I let myself step inside it as if it already existed: summer, three in the afternoon, the pavement hotter out there; here, under the shadows, the air drops two degrees and the light turns gentle. I can hear a local band tes-ting their sound in the background. A child runs by; his laughter crosses through columns of shadow and water. An older woman sits with her granddaughter; they share a bottle of water, and the girl dips her hand into the fountain, flicking droplets toward the sun, forming a tiny arc that only they celebrate. Two teenagers on skate-boards make a straight stretch, brake near a reflecting pool, stare at their reflection, and, without planning to, take a picture of themsel-ves. A man in work clothes listens to stern words on the phone, hangs up, exhales, and gazes at the light climbing up a green wall. That's what we're drawing, I think. Not a box for selling. A gathering place that, gently, gives us back the desire to be.

And then, as it often happens, the present opens to let an old echo in.

Amarillo, "High School".

Mr. Collins stands in front of my chaotic drawing—lines that, to me, are an entire universe.

"Simplify, Matt. Make it understandable. The rest is noise."

The classroom smells like a crowd and chalk dust. Outside, the Panhandle wind pushes clouds against an impatient sky. On my page, lines rise and fall, staircases lead to no doors, and doors open onto slanted courtyards; red shadows cast as if it were always late afternoon; there's a bridge suspended over nothing that reminds me of a dream.

To me, it all has an order—an order I can't explain without ruining it. Collins steps closer, pinching the edge of my paper between two fingers, like someone holding something they don't want to stain.

"Nobody understands this," he says, not even glancing at the rest of the class. "Less is more."

Two small laughs sound from the back—a chair scrapes. I feel my cheeks burn; the pencil feels like a nail in my hand.

I look at my lines; I still love them. I think of saying that "less is more" belongs to those who already have everything—that for me, less sometimes takes the words away. But I say nothing.

Collins slaps the desk with a gesture that's supposed to be pedagogical.

"Simplify," he repeats, and places my paper on the desk with a lukewarm gesture that hurts more than a reprimand.

Breaking a pencil is easy. Just press it right in the center and twist. I learned it that day.

The graphite snapped in a diagonal, the wood splintered. No one noticed.

In that small gesture, a wound took root—one that still bleeds whenever someone says "simplify" as if it were a commandment.

The next scene, I see from the outside, as if my eyes belonged to someone else: me in my room that afternoon, closing the door quietly.

My mother calls me to dinner. I say I'm not hungry, that I'll come down later. The drawing waits on the desk. I fold it once, twice, three times—each crease an act of betrayal. The paper gives a dry crack.

I tear it up. The pieces lie like dead birds on the wood. I try to fit them back into a single shape. I can't.

I gather them up and hide them in a shoebox I slide under the bed, as if keeping them there would preserve them from something.

I lie there, staring at the ceiling. A train moves past outside, its whistle cutting through the night. In that long sound, I make a promise I've kept ever since: never to give up my lines so others can sleep in peace.

I find myself back in my office chair. My fingers tremble slightly. I touch the edge of the monitor. I repeat, almost under my breath: VitaPlaza wasn't born from a passing whim. It was born from watching this city grow the way a knotted plant grows—stretching, straining, always reaching for light. It was born from knowing that the northern metroplex doesn't need another perfectly air conditioned box with windowless corridors, but rather a gesture that embraces the sky as its roof and learns from it without trying to domesticate it.

It was born from countless visits to Frisco, where I saw families pushing strollers along sidewalks without shade, teenagers taking refuge in a store's air conditioning because there was no bench, and people wanting to be together but not finding a place to do so. It was born from the conviction—romantic, perhaps, or simply practical—that commerce thrives better when the place has a soul. Not the other way around.

I straighten up. I zoom in on the blueprint, finding the central corridor, the line of trees, and the interplay between the water platform and the steps. There it is—the outline I can't move from: the heart. The rest can be adjusted—a wall section here, a plant species better suited to the late frost, the length of a sail, the diameter of a duct. Those can be negotiable. The gesture cannot.

I wonder—just to be honest with myself—if there's a version of "simplify" that doesn't hurt. Maybe there is a way: refining without emptying. When one less line makes the intention clearer. But what Carver asked for wasn't refinement. It was to strip the soul out and then ask us to smile. "It's a mall, not a park." A soundless laugh escapes me. I sometimes wonder why it's so hard for some people to understand that people buy better when they first feel like people.

I lean back. The chair squeaks briefly. Through the glass, I see Allison talking with Samuel at his desk; Samuel holds his coffee with both hands, as if to gather courage. I should call them in, close the door again, and tell them we'll redo whatever needs redoing without betraying our ideals. But first, I need to shake off the anger before it turns into an argument.

I don't want to go to battle with a sword forged out of adolescence. I want to go in with reasons—and with my body aligned.

I press my fingers against the edge of the table and leave them there. I think about Mr. Collins, and I'd love to invite him now to walk through a built VitaPlaza: to guide him under the canopies on a sun-heavy day, to seat him beside a reflecting pool at dusk, to let him hear how the noise fades barely ten feet away, to show him a child running and stopping to touch an almost invisible mist. To tell him, "This, too, makes sense." Without pride. Maybe it would. Maybe not. It doesn't matter anymore. I don't do this for Collins. I do it—I try to remind myself of this when frustration closes in—for the people I haven't met yet: for the lady who will come with a book no one else wants to read; for the teenager who hates Saturdays because he never knows what to do with his hands; for those who work in a store twelve-hour shifts and need a real shaded bench where they can sit and eat without swallowing the sun.

I return to the model. I picture a January winter: the canopies drawn tight like sails, the water still, a cold breath in the air. I picture a May afternoon with the first hint of heat, mist alight, shadows moving like a clock without numbers. I picture nights with low lights and local musicians; small vendors with carts that smell of cotton candy and tacos; a couple arguing softly and reconciling without noticing because a child suddenly laughs too loudly by the fountain. I picture a youth soccer team crossing the corridor with muddy uniforms, heading straight for the ice-cream stand. I picture a place where people can linger. And lingering, in cities that grow like this one, is a luxury we still need.

I think about Carver. He is not my enemy. He is someone who sees numbers that I do not see today. But he has a flaw I already know: he believes anything living is superfluous and complicated. Part of my work is to remind him that the living pays the rent. The shade from a canopy in August is not only relief, it is the difference between an overworked air conditioner and an open space that stays cool on its own. The sound of water attracts people because it calms the body, inviting them to stay longer. A wall of plants isn't a 'green' backdrop for photos but the site's own breathing system— proof that it's a place meant to be lived in, not merely passed through.

I get up and walk to the whiteboard. With the marker, I write scattered words that, to anyone else, would seem like random things: "heart," "living space," "summer heat," "space to relax," "sounds of community," "belonging," "hidden shade," "not a cash box," "Frisco—new spaces." They are keywords that help me understand and remember. I go back to the desk.

I open a new email. I write in the subject: "VitaPlaza—Non-negotiable essence / Possible adjustments". Below, in the body of the email—still unsent—I write for Allison and Samuel:

> Let's find a way to adjust costs without touching what makes VitaPlaza unique. The essentials are not negotiable: the structural green walls, water as the heart of the space, and the shade that shelters without overpowering.
>
> I suggest we review together:
>
> Canopies: explore alternative paths and supports to reduce steel use without sacrificing essential shade.
>
> Reflecting pools: keep the main feature while optimizing the design. Perhaps we can play with geometry or more fluid perimeters—something like a golf 'fairway'—that preserves the same visual breadth without requiring as much water.
>
> Planters and greenery walls: look for over-

laps or areas where we can reduce secondary elements, but without sacrificing the walls that bring life and breathing space to the project.

I'll provide arguments on microclimate and acoustics, focusing on energy savings, thermal regulation, and the impact on user experience. I need the same level of precision from both of you: Allison, on how we communicate this to the client and uphold our narrative; Samuel, on the calculations and technical efficiencies that support each adjustment.

The essence is untouchable. But we can still find a way to prove that what is alive is not a luxury—it's a wise investment. And VitaPlaza must stand as proof of that.

—Matt

I don't send it. Not yet. I get up and look out the window. On the street, the wind stirs a newspaper page that someone left behind. It dances, turns, leans against a wheel, drifts off again, reaches the corner, and disappears. Those are the paths where energy escapes when someone tries to lock it in. If Carver wants walls, I want openings. If he wants boxes, I want plazas. That's the battle.

I sit back down and close my eyes for a moment. Taking stock: my jaw has unclenched, my shoulders have eased, my breathing has found a gentler rhythm. I'm still angry, yes—but beneath the anger there's something steadier, a conviction I first learned in my youth, now written in different words. I murmur it to myself, slowly, like a prayer without a religion: I will not simplify what breathes. If something needs refining, we refine. If something needs adjusting, we adjust. If something needs defending, we defend.

I open my eyes and press send. On the screen, VitaPlaza is still a drawing. In my mind, it is already full of people.

Samuel is already in the project room when I walk in. It's barely 9:40, yet he looks as if he's been there for hours. On his screen, an energetic 3D model is open—blue and orange arrows shifting like invisible currents, as if the computer were breathing through them. I don't have to ask; I know he spent the night chasing the numbers that could prove what I call intuition.

"Look at this," he says, without turning, pointing with his stylus. "The green walls lower the average temperature in the central corridor by 15 to 20 percent. Less trapped heat means less air conditioning for the shops. Translated into bills, that translates to thousands of dollars a year in bills."

I listen in silence. Sometimes I'm struck by how much I need sentences like that—not poetry, not metaphors, just percentages that survive on a spreadsheet. Samuel has that skill: turning my chaos into figures that don't lose their power. What to me feels like skin and shade becomes, to him, kilowatts and dollars. And suddenly, the living no longer seems like a luxury.

Allison walks in as she always does, without announcing herself. She's carrying two cups of coffee and sets one in front of me without a glance, as if the gesture itself had been precisely measured. She takes her seat at the table, opens her laptop, and her fingers start flying, as though they were following the lines of an invisible speech already written.

"Listen to this," she says, without looking up: "Every dollar invested in climate comfort yields three in permanence. People buy more when they stay longer. And people stay longer when a place feels like it belongs to them." She pauses, takes a sip. "It's not an expense; it's an investment in permanence. That's how we're going to present it."

I nod slowly. I realize that the word "belonging" has already taken root in my head, but now it sounds different, more polished. Allison knows how to wrap the same words in a different light. If I say "water calms bodies", it can sound poetic. If she says "water increases permanence", it becomes a sellable argument. We need both of us.

I take a sheet of tracing paper and begin sketching with a pencil over the printed blueprint: a circle in the center for the main reflecting pool, broken lines for projected shadows, irregular rectangles for the green walls.

"The heart is not to be touched," I say quietly, almost to myself. Then, firmer: "What we can do is surround that heart with smart adjustments."

In the margin, I write: Canopies: alternate paths and supports.

"We could test different tension levels," Samuel adds. "With a structural redesign, we might save 10 percent of the steel."

I nod, but raise my hand, crossing my index and middle fingers as if to catch an idea before it slips away.

"And let's not forget this," I say. "We don't need to cover 100 percent of the area with canvas to create shade. That was never the goal." I pause, studying the blueprint, my fingers resting on the glass. "What we do cover is 100 percent of the rain. If a storm hits, no one gets wet. That's the difference: here, the sky stays open, but the water never interrupts the life of the plaza."

Samuel nods, adjusting the screen.

"Exactly. It's a design that lets the light through but keeps out what truly disturbs. I'll write it that way in the notes."

Allison translates it immediately into words:

"An invisible roof that protects without enclosing." Even Carver will get that.

I jot down: Reflecting pools: same visual span, less real volume.

"I'm thinking of more fluid geometries," I say. "Something like a golf fairway—it looks more expansive, but actually uses less water."

Samuel smiles.

"I can model that in a hydric simulator."

Next, I write: Planters: remove duplicates, keep key walls.

Allison looks up.

"I'd phrase it this way: We optimize without losing the essence. If we say it outright, Carver won't see it as stubbornness, but as professionalism."

I lean back in my chair for a moment, watching them both bend over the table—Samuel scribbling calculations in the margins, Allison fine-tuning phrases on her screen. And it hits me: I'm not alone. The weight I carried back from Frisco dissolves here, because between the three of us, we're weaving a language made of soul and numbers, emotion and precision.

"The living is not a luxury," I murmur. "It's a smart investment."

Allison lifts her eyes from the keyboard and meets my gaze, like someone recognizing a title.

"I'm going to put that on the first slide."

Samuel says nothing, but his pencil continues marking percentages along the edge of my drawing. That's his way of agreeing.

We work for nearly two hours without lifting our heads. The table ends up covered in my sketches, Samuel's efficiency charts, and Allison's underlined phrases. It might look like chaos, but it's really a symphony of languages finding harmony.

At one point, Allison sets her laptop aside and looks straight at me.

"Matt, what's happening with Carver isn't personal. He just needs to know that every dollar he spends will come back multiplied. That fear is what we have to turn into trust. He has to understand they hired us for authenticity. And authenticity may be costly—but it pays off."

"What if he doesn't listen?" I ask.

"Then he'll listen to Excel. Samuel's got the facts."

Samuel smiles with a shy smile that rarely surfaces.

"I've built comparative energy-consumption models. If the green walls disappear, cooling costs rise by 20 percent. That's undeniable."

I look at him. He lowers his eyes, as always, but what I feel is gratitude—not for the numbers themselves, but for the fact that someone took the time to back up my vision with science.

"Alright," I say, taking a deep breath. "We don't compromise on the essence. We just adjust the form."

Allison closes her laptop with a soft snap.

"That's the narrative. And with the right narrative, Matt, even Carver can change his mind."

I glance at the whiteboard. My scattered words from the morning are still there—heart, shade, belonging. They no longer look like isolated cries. Now, they're part of a plan.

We stand up almost at the same time. Samuel gathers the papers; Allison picks up the empty cups. I walk over to the rendering again—this time with less anger, more clarity. VitaPlaza is still what we dreamed. Perhaps with less steel, maybe with water used more wisely, but untouched where it matters.

As we leave the room, Allison pats my arm.

"Breathe. This time we're not going to war alone. We're going to make it."

And I believe it. For the first time in days, I truly do.

The road to Frisco stretches long and flat, as if the highway itself wanted to give me time to sort through the noise in my head. I'm driving; Allison sits in the passenger seat, scrolling through notes on her tablet, while Samuel is in the back, leafing through the blueprints he probably knows by heart. We don't talk much. The silence fills with the hum of the air conditioning and the soft, rhythmic tapping of Allison's fingers on the screen. I grip the wheel harder than I need to. Now and then, Samuel clears his throat, like someone preparing for an exam.

The mid-morning sun beats down without mercy. The air vibrates with a palpable tension, thick and heavy. Each ray falls like hot metal, searing the skin slowly, without pity. In the distance, machines level the ground—mechanical arms rising and falling in an almost animal rhythm, biting into the ground until it yields to dust and gravel. The metallic clatter blends with the growl of diesel engines and the dull thud of collapsing soil. Here, in this barren stretch that still smells of warm clay and fuel, someone is waiting for us to build a future.

I roll down the window a bit, but all that comes in is a blast of dry air, heavy with dust, that burns more than it cools. I think, almost aloud: I don't want a plaza where people feel this, this infernal heat that forces you to rush from one air-conditioned space to another, as if the city can only be experienced indoors.

No. VitaPlaza will be different. The contrast is etched in my mind: today, this arid, burning stretch of land; tomorrow—if we stand our ground—a heart of shade and water that will make Frisco feel like a different place.

Allison and Samuel watch me from the back seat as I park in front of the construction trailers—those prefabricated offices that usually feel impersonal, but here, in the middle of the dust, rise like the first promise of what's to come.

The construction office is a white trailer, but Carver has made sure it looks otherwise. Plywood panels cover the walls, there's a scent of new carpet, and the air conditioning is set to a chilly, artificial temperature. A brand-new conference table gleams in the center. It's not a makeshift cubicle—it looks like a real building, as if even in something temporary, he needed to command respect. Irony: we're here to talk about authenticity, in a place pretending to be something it's not.

We take our seats. Outside, the ground continues to shift and rumble. Carver starts the meeting in his impeccable gray suit, a shiny watch catching the trailer's artificial light. He doesn't smile. He doesn't waste time.

"Remember, we have to cut costs," he says, as if the word itself were a lifeline we should all cling to.

His finger taps the table in a steady rhythm. Before him lies a spreadsheet filled with numbers—columns in green and red, percentages that leave no room for birds or shade.

I watch him without interrupting. I think about how easy it is for him to reduce a living space to boxes with black borders. Before I can speak, Samuel steps in.

"The green walls lower the temperature in the central corridor by 15 to 20 percent," he says. "That means less air conditioning in

105

each store, lower utility bills, and higher long-term profitability." He flips through the pages with the calm assurance of someone who knows the science backs him up.

Carver leans forward.

"But those walls cost a fortune upfront."

Allison cuts in—gentle but firm.

"It's an investment, not an expense. Think about it: a closed shopping center needs a massive central system to cool every corridor, plus the individual air conditioning for each store. That's millions a year in electricity bills. With our design, the plaza cools itself. The green walls regulate temperature. The reflecting pools help cool the air. The canopies block direct sunlight. Your clients won't feel the heat we felt walking across this site." She pauses, looking him straight in the eye. "It's not a luxury. It's natural engineering. And when nature is well designed, it pays the rent."

She lets the phrase fall into the air like a stone dropped into a pond. The silence ripples outward in slow circles. Samuel nods slightly, adjusting an energy-consumption chart with his finger—kilowatts, dollars, percentages. Science backing up what, for me, has always been intuition: that the living doesn't just decorate, it saves.

I remain silent for a moment, letting their voices build a bridge. My hand moves along the edge of the table, feeling the cool grain of the wood beneath my fingers. Then I straighten up in my chair, rest both palms on the surface, and meet Carver's eyes without blinking.

"We were hired to create living spaces," I say at last. "If what you wanted was a box of concrete," I say, "you called the wrong team." My voice sounds steadier than I feel—no tremor, no edge, just as a flat line laid across the table.

Carver sits still. His finger stops its rhythmic tapping. A short silence follows, heavier than any argument. Outside, the screech of an excavator cuts through the air. Inside, every breath seems to hold.

The sun outside continues to blaze, but in here the heat was of another kind—the kind that builds in long hours around a table where no one wants to yield. Carver hadn't come alone; he brought two advisors who looked as if they'd been designed to stare at spreadsheets until they bled. They spoke about margins, CAPEX, and ROI—acronyms repeated like mantras.

Samuel responded with his own numbers, figures he didn't invent: kilowatts saved, thousands shaved off energy bills, degrees of temperature reduced. Each sentence was a solid brick supporting my intuition. Allison wrapped those facts in discourse, turning figures into images: more dwell time, higher sales, stronger customer loyalty. I listened to them both, and at times it felt like my only task was to stay upright—to keep Carver from confusing austerity with absence.

It wasn't easy.

There were moments when I thought we were about to lose half of what made the project alive.

Carver drummed his fingers, insisting that cuts were inevitable, that "details" were eating up the budget. I met his gaze without blinking, remembering my broken drawings in Amarillo, that word splintering in my mind: "simplify."

There were long silences, with sheets of paper passed back and forth as fast as the wind, glances searching for cracks. Hours went by like that—crossed arguments, diagram over diagram, voices raised just enough to be heard without becoming shouts. Outside, the machines kept working. Inside, we were trying to save the essence of a dream.

"Fine," Carver says at last, settling back in his chair. "We'll keep the main walls, the central reflecting pool, and the strategic canopies. But I need you to optimize the secondary elements—less water volume, fewer duplicate planters, more efficient structures."

I nod slowly. It's not a total victory, but it's not a defeat either. We've saved the heart of it: the gardens that breathe, the water that soothes, the shade that protects without enclosing. The rest can be adjusted.

The meeting concludes with quick signatures, and the agreements are jotted down in the minutes. Carver packs away his spreadsheet. Samuel gathers his blueprints and reaches for his calculator. Allison glances at me, the kind that says quietly: "You're not alone. We're a team."

When we step out of the trailer, the sun hits us full in the face. The ground still vibrates with the machines. I stop for a moment in the dust, letting the light burn my skin, and think—this is the real setting of the project. Not a spreadsheet in a trailer, but the heat, the wind, the life that will someday move through this place. I don't want anyone in VitaPlaza to endure this relentless heat. I like the air itself to change when they step inside—to receive them, not drive them away. That's what we fought for today.

Allison and Samuel wanted to celebrate. They suggested a quick dinner, a toast somewhere, but I asked them to give me the space to celebrate alone. There were no objections—there never are. They agreed right away, as if they understood that, for me, silence is also a kind of celebration.

So, I ended up here, in my usual refuge. The contrast with Frisco is stark: there, the dust and the sun that felt like it wanted to strip your skin; here, the golden dimness of low lamps, soft jazz brushing the air, the calm of a place I know by heart.

James, behind the bar, recognizes me instantly. Without asking, he serves me my wine—a dark, full-bodied red that's become part of the ritual.

I settle into my usual seat at the far right, with the wall behind me and the whole room in view. From here, I can see everything without being seen. The table glows in a small circle of light, as if that intimate halo existed only to contain my own exhaustion. This time I haven't come entirely alone: I've brought my notebook. I place it beside me, closed, as if it were keeping me company in silence until I decide to open it. Tonight, I want to write away from home, to test how my voice sounds in a different place.

The steak arrives right on time—a New York strip steak, medium well-cooked. The first bite is more than food; it's certainty. The tenderness of the meat, the smoky aroma, the seasoning, the contrast with the wine—everything else—Carver, his advisors, the spreadsheets, the tapping of his finger on the table—fades away, dissolving into the background. For once, I allow myself to eat slowly, savoring every detail, every sip of wine, as if calm itself could be served on a plate.

I take the last sip and set the glass aside. I press the napkin lightly to my lips. I lift the empty glass slightly toward James, and he—who already knows my silences—nods from behind the bar. In seconds, he refills it, and that small gesture settles me inside. Now I'm ready. Only then do I draw the notebook closer.

I leave it open for a moment on the bar as if it needs to breathe with me before it fills up. My fingers run along the spine, feeling the weight of all the previous pages, the days when writing was catharsis—and sometimes punishment. Tonight, there is no punishment. Tonight, there is only space.

I write slowly, the black ink flowing steadily:

"Chaos cannot be simplified; it must be lived."

I pause. I look at the words on the page the way one studies a wound that has already healed. And suddenly, I think of Elena. She never knew this place.

I never shared this refuge with her. If I ever have the chance to be with someone again, I promise myself I won't hide these places anymore. I promise to share every corner that holds me, every space that saves me. The thought lingers for a second, then slips away.

I look up: the room murmurs in low tones, cutlery brushing softly, glasses chiming gently. No one looks at me. No one expects anything from me. And in that murmur, I feel something close to belonging.

I close the notebook slowly. Rest my hand on the cover, as if sealing a private vow. I smile, just a little. This time, I didn't betray my vision. This time, I defended what is alive. And though the world outside still runs on numbers and concessions, here, in this corner of golden light, I let myself taste the fragile certainty of a small victory.

I didn't win everything. But I defended what matters. And that, in a world that insists on silencing life with dead formulas, is enough.

In the end, chaos makes room to live.

7 Echoes of Childhood

"It is only with the heart that one can see rightly;
what is essential is invisible to the eye."
— Antoine de Saint-Exupéry, *The Little Prince*

The email arrives with a blunt subject line:

```
"Urgent review. Immediate adjustments."
```

No greeting, no sign-off. Carver never uses more words than necessary, as if every extra character cost him money.

I open the message, and there it is, black letters on a white background:

```
"Simplify. Steel costs are out of control. I
need alternatives. No frills."
```

I take a deep breath. The air conditioner whirrs in the corner of the office—a constant vibration that drills into me more than usual today. The air feels colder than it should, as if it's trying to pierce through the skin and reach the bones. There's a pile of paper clips on my desk, and I find myself lining them up without thinking: one, two, three, four. I set them in a row, spin them, and realign them again. The noise outside pushes me inward.

VitaPlaza is only beginning, and already it feels like a weight I've carried for years. The canopies—those wings I envisioned as a refuge from the relentless Texas sun—are now called "excessive," "unnecessary," "complicated." The numbers rise and fall on the Excel sheets they send me each week, but what matters most doesn't fit in any cell: pleasant shade, breathable air, a welcoming gesture.

This morning, I got a call, and the words are still echoing in my head. We'd been reviewing the structural loads with the chief engineer.

Travis Patterson, head of structures, his voice neutral, like someone reading a medical report:

"This is too complicated, Matt."

"Complicated." The word lingers, vibrating like a metallic echo. He could have said "costly" or "technically challenging," and I would have taken it better. But "complicated" lands differently—it digs in, as if it weren't just about the project but about me.

I try to focus on the rendering projected on the wall. The image is sharp: the canopies stretched wide, their lines taut and graceful between slender columns. To me, they're almost music—lines that respond to the wind, shadows tracing geometry on the floor. To Carver—and now to Travis—they're only red numbers on a bleeding budget.

My fingers tap against the edge of the keyboard. I count my breaths: one, two, three, four. The whirr of the air conditioner grows until it fills the room. The paper clips I had lined up lie scattered again, and I catch myself rearranging them, as if in that small act I could regain control.

I stand up abruptly from my chair and walk to the conference room, where I know Allison and Samuel are reviewing other submissions. I open the door without knocking.

"I need us to look at the canopies now!" I say—maybe louder than necessary.

Allison lifts her eyes from her laptop. Not a flicker of surprise. She just nods and closes the file she was working on.

"Let's go to the table, Matt."

Samuel is already on his feet, notebook of calculations in hand— his ever-present one. He always carries it, even though he runs everything on software. It's his way of translating numbers to paper, of grounding what, for me, are floating intuitions.

I spread the printed blueprints across the table under the projector's beam. I point to the support spots, the tensions, the projections. My voice rushes out, as if I had to empty everything jammed in my head at once.

"We can shorten the anchor lengths if we use the shop roofs as direct supports—here and here." I trace two corners with my finger. "That would save us the need for additional foundations."

Samuel leans over, pencil in hand, and begins sketching on the sheet.

"That would mean reinforcing the slabs," he says, already running the numbers in his head.

"Yes, but it's cheaper to reinforce than to lay new foundations. And if we shift part of the anchoring toward the facades, we can hide the system within the building's skin."

Samuel mutters to himself, barely audible.

"Let's see… if I fix this column here… anchor this tension rod there… the loads will distribute better." He makes a few quick notes. "Let me run more detailed projections later, but at first glance, it looks feasible."

Allison follows every word in silence. She notes something in her notebook.

"And the steel?" she asks, calm as ever.

"We can look into using thinner tension rods, as long as the loads allow it," Samuel says, not lifting his head.

"We can also play with height," he adds. "If we lower a few feet in certain spots, we reduce tension and cut down on steel without sacrificing shade."

"Exactly," I say. "And if we keep the membrane's sinuous design, the resistance distributes more evenly. The curve helps the structure—it doesn't complicate it."

I can hear myself speaking too fast, as if chased by an invisible clock. Allison notices. She stops me with a single phrase in a low tone:

"Breathe, Matt."

I lean on the table for a moment, pressing my palms against the paper as if to steady myself. I take a deep breath. My mind doesn't shut off; I keep seeing alternatives, paths, formulas that may not even exist. But at least I have the best team with me.

Samuel finally looks up, his glasses catching the reflection of the sketch-filled blueprint.

"If we move these supports to the rooftops, we'll cut foundation costs by 15 percent. It won't be enough for Carver, but it's a solid argument."

Allison speaks up.

"And let's not forget something—Carver already approved a budget. The rise in steel prices isn't on us. If he wants to make deeper cuts now, he's breaking his own agreement." She flips through her notes calmly, though her voice stays firm. "We need to analyze if the adjustments we're proposing now will be enough to offset that increase. What we're not going to do is play his game—cutting all the canopies just because steel went up. Maybe he's using that as an excuse to get his way."

She pauses and looks straight at me.

"So yes, we'll come in with solutions—but also with a clear limit. What he needs are solid arguments, not poetry. I'll take care of the presentation: cost savings, material efficiency, long-term sustainability. That's what he can sell."

I nod. I look again at the canopies projected on the wall, at the blueprints spread out before us, now covered with pencil marks and notes. I picture how the changes will look in the next rendering. In my mind, they're still wings, refuge, shade. For them, they're numbers. But between the three of us, we've carved out a small opening: not to abandon the idea, but to shape it so it survives. And in that contrast—between wings and figures—I know there's still space for the project to breathe.

I sink into the conference chair. The air conditioner keeps humming. Carver will keep sending his blunt emails. But now, even in my exhaustion, I feel a thread of connection. I'm not defending this alone.

And yet, Travis Patterson's voice still follows me:

"This is too complicated, Matt."

That adjective opens an old door. The present overlaps with a memory that never quite fades: a family table, voices overwhelming everything, a child holding up a drawing no one wants to see.

The door to memory opens without resistance.

A Sunday from my childhood in Amarillo.

The dining table is larger than the house needs—dark wood covered with a plastic tablecloth that catches the ceiling light like a small domestic sun. A fan spins slowly, pushing the smell of stewed meat, warm bread, and fried onions through the room. The drinking glasses are heavy; when set down, they make a dull thud that blends with the clinking of silverware and the continuous murmur of overlapping voices.

My parents sit at the head of the table—upright, smiling—with the tired joy of people holding the day together. To their right, the family friends—the affectionate "uncles"—fill the far end, laughing loudly, gesturing as they tell stories, piling food onto their plates as if hunger itself were a shared joke.

Their four children move through the place like a pack—getting up for soda, coming back with laughter hanging from their shoulders, pushing chairs without apology. The house seems made for them.

To my left, my older brother glows with the confidence of someone who always knows when to speak. There's a kind of key in his voice—every time he uses it, everyone turns to listen.

To my right, my younger sister receives gentle questions from the adults—How was school? What did you learn?—and each of her answers is met with a quick burst of praise, a "How lovely!" or "How smart!" They applaud small things, and for a second, the air itself seems to light up.

My hands stay under the table, holding my drawing as if it were a nervous little animal. It's a house that doesn't exist: a house with huge windows, a courtyard with water to quiet the noise, a porch shaped like an embrace.

In one corner, I've scribbled shadows falling in diagonal lines, like clocks. The materials aren't explicit—just imagined textures: stone with memory, wood that doesn't pretend to be anything else. I look at it and feel something I can't define—a belonging to a form that doesn't quite exist yet.

"Did you see Eli play today?" one of the "uncles" shouts, stadium-voiced. "He's going to be a quarterback, you'll see."

The adults laugh. My brother talks about solving something in class; they listen as if he were reading the newspaper. My sister gets sauce on her face, and Mom cleans her up with a napkin—her gesture tender and reassuring. The uncles' children compete to tell TV jokes, two at a time, and somehow someone still understands and laughs. The fan murmurs above us all. The tablecloth has a thin blue line running through it like a river. I keep an eye on it so I won't get lost.

"I made a drawing," I say—at first only in my head. I rehearse the tone, the pause, the exact phrasing so it will fall into place naturally.

I try to raise my voice.

"I... made a drawing."

My father glances at me and nods with a brief smile, while one of the "uncles" dives into another story—something about work, a stubborn client, an office joke. The table begins to spin on its own axis again. A glass clinks, a chair scrapes the floor, someone asks for more bread.

I wait for an opening. There are always openings, I tell myself. You just have to find them.

"Look," I try again, "it's a house..."

My older brother delivers a punchline that draws laughter. My sister shows a drawing she made at school—a sun with enormous eyes and a flower shaped like a face—and everyone leans in to see it. "How pretty!" "Show it to your aunt!" They touch her hair as if applauding in silence.

"Very good, son," my mother says to me—her affection arriving and fading in a single breath—"but listen to your brother."

I obey. Not because I want to, but because the phrase has the tone of an instruction that existed long before it was spoken.

Laughter slides across the table like oil, and some of it spills onto my plate, making it heavier. The fork in my hand feels like lead. The meat is getting cold around the edges. The drawing is getting sweaty between my fingers. I think that if I pull it out now, no one will look at it—it would be like setting a live bird down in the middle of a road.

I breathe. I count the rhythm of the fan: one, two, three, four turns. I watch the shadow of the blades. I trace the seam of the tablecloth with my fingertip; it's rough, imperfect, real. The blue line seems to tell me the same thing: move forward, even if the noise doesn't stop.

"And what about you?" the affectionate "aunt" asks with a smile that sweeps across everyone. "Did you play with your cousins?"

I nod, with a gesture that neither lies nor confirms anything. I think—no. I'd rather stay watching how the shadows moved across the living room floor, how the afternoon light drew triangles and then twisted shapes. My game was measuring time by the fall of one line over another. How do you explain that without sounding weird? How do you describe a game that has no ball, no hiding place?

"He's got talent," my father says, looking at my brother. "I said it when he was little. He talks like an adult. And he's great at leading the team."

Everyone nods. Someone raises a glass—water, soda, it doesn't matter. The word "talent" bounces and lands where it always does.

I feel the drawing stirring, as if the paper wanted to breathe. I slide it a single inch out from its hiding place under the table. The corners brush my knees. I slip it back in. Some decisions happen in the smallest of spaces: one inch of paper can be either defeat or victory.

The pack of four cousins starts a race down the hallway. They come back sweaty, laughing, breathless. One of them bumps my chair and mumbles an apology without looking. Behind them lingers a smell of grass, cheap soap, summer.

"Come on, princess, tell us again about your teacher," the

"aunt" says, turning to my sister.

They listen to her. They celebrate her. I listen too; she's talking about a flower drawing she pinned to the classroom corkboard. The corkboard is beautiful, I think, because it takes in whatever is placed on it—maps, flowers, notes, mistakes. A place that always makes room.

My mother serves me more food. I say "thank you," and she squeezes my shoulder—quickly, precisely, like someone setting a lamp just right. There was no lack of love. What was missing was something else—a kind of ear for my inner voice.

The uncle imitates a sports announcer; everyone laughs. The fan no longer cools—it slices the air into thick pieces. The tablecloth wrinkles where I rest my elbow—a fold that looks like a mountain to me. I could draw it right now—one line rising, another holding it up, a valley where silence might rest. I pull the drawing halfway out. Almost. Almost.

My brother says something else. My father looks at him as if he were looking in a mirror. My sister shows another small thing that draws a chorus of "Aww." I commit to precision: I trace an invisible diagonal along the paper's edge with my fingernail—my secret ruler.

"I'm going to the bathroom," I lie.

No one stops me. I walk slowly down the hallway, the drawing folded against my stomach, held with the care one gives to a bird that shouldn't wake up.

I go into my room. The door closes, shutting out two laughs, three questions, and a toast. Inside, there's a comforting calm. The bed recites the dust of the afternoon. On the desk lie other papers: façades without people, courtyards waiting for their sound, notes I can't tell if they're words or materials.

I open the shoebox. Dozens of folded sheets of paper—a map of all the things I never said. Each page is a piece of me.

Some lines are broken halfway because they were folded too many times. Some doors lead nowhere—yet. There is water drawn in pencil, shadows traced with the edge of an eraser. Hope, hidden in the drawings, crumpled.

I place today's drawing with the others, as if hiding it from something I can't define. The box sounds hollow when it closes. I slide it under the bed.

I stand for a moment, listening to the muffled sound of the table from here. It sounds like the sea when you press your ear to a shell—just as beautiful, and just as distant. I run my fingers over the surface of the desk. It's warm—a kind of warmth that asks for nothing.

I sit down. I open a new blank sheet of paper. I try to draw a different table—one where everyone could sit without needing to raise their voices. I add a long bench with a gentle curve; above it, a lamp that doesn't glare, that doesn't feel like interrogation. I place many windows to turn shouts into murmurs. I open a space toward a courtyard where the air can move without pushing. I leave a place for whoever arrives late and doesn't want to explain.

My hand is shaking a little. Not with fear; with that strange excitement that comes when something is starting to exist. The paper is breathing. I am too.

A knock at the door. My mother's voice comes clear, without the foam of laughter.

"Are you all right, sweetheart?"

"Yes," I say. "I'm coming."

She doesn't open. She doesn't come in. She leaves me the space, as if she somehow knew I needed it. I hear her walk back to the table. The noise rises for a moment, then fades. I imagine dessert has been served. The house smells of cinnamon now.

I look again at the paper. The table I've just drawn doesn't look like the one downstairs—but it doesn't deny it, either. It's another possibility. I touch the corner of the paper with my finger-tip, as if I could bless something. And in a voice so low that no one can take the word from me, I promise:

Someday, my drawings will be seen.

I close the paper carefully, like someone folding a freshly pressed shirt. I rest my forehead against the edge of the desk. I count the turns of the ceiling fan: one, two, three, four. My chest loosens slightly, as if the air has finally found the right way in.

I return to the dining room. The aunts and uncles are talking about next Sunday at the park, while the cousins are laughing and arguing over who gets the window seat in the car.

My older brother receives a pat on the back from my father; my sister laughs with her mouth full, and my mother looks at her with that blend of scolding and tenderness that heals everything. I was neither on one side nor the other. No one asks about my drawing. It is as if I'd been left on a different shore.

I sit back in my chair. The tablecloth is no longer a mountain to me—it's a whole range I know I can cross. The cold glass dampens my fingers. I count to four and drink. The world remains noisy, as always, but now between the noise and me there's a paper that says "still."

Someone asks if I want more bread. I say no, thank you. I'm full in a different way.

The ceiling lamp casts a perfect circle of light over the center of the table. I remember how I used to sit mesmerized, watching that light spill down like a yellow puddle. The steam from the food would rise and blur it, as if invisible shadows were floating in the air. I didn't understand it then—I just thought it was strange and beautiful.

My mother glances at me out of the corner of her eye, as if she's guessed at least a fragment of my world. She smiles. I smile back. That's enough for me.

The fan spins once more. Outside the window, the spring sky stretches into long clouds, like white ribbons someone forgot to gather. The ribbons move to the rhythm of a wind we can't see.

At the table, they ask for coffee. I don't want any. What I want is to go back to my room, open the box, take out the papers, and keep drawing—without noise, without anyone to overlook me.

But I stay. I eat a piece of bread. I half-listen to a story. I hand a napkin to the person who asks for one. I do what's done at tables. And at the same time, inside, I begin to imagine.

The murmur of the table in Amarillo fades, but doesn't disappear completely. I can still hear my sister laughing, my mother saying, "Listen to your brother." Only now those voices come mixed with others: the electric hum of the projector, the shuffle of papers across the table, the insistent click of a pen someone forgot to stop. I'm back in the conference room, but the wound from childhood remains open—covered only by a thin layer of cold air.

Allison sits across from me, bent over her laptop. Her fingers move quickly, almost silently, as if they know my head is still echoing too loudly. Beside her, Samuel draws short lines in his notebook. He talks to himself in a low murmur that might seem trivial to anyone else, but to me it sounds like the construction of an invisible scaffold:

"If we shift this support point... the angle changes, the load distributes... yes, it could work here."

I watch his hands: a line, another, an arrow, a number. It's the mathematical translation of what I imagine as wings. Where I see shade and calm, he sees forces and tension. And I'm grateful for that, though it's hard to admit—without his calculations, my wings would never take off.

Allison looks up for a moment and, without saying a word, pushes a cup of coffee toward me. She doesn't offer it ceremoniously— just sets it down near my hand, like someone placing a stone to mark a path. Something about the gesture's simplicity shakes me. At the table in Amarillo, no one saw me; here, at least, someone says without words: you're here, and I see you.

"Samuel," Allison says, breaking the silence, her voice firm but calm. "Remind me of the energy savings with the canopies."

Samuel adjusts his glasses and flips through his notebook.

"Twenty-five percent less energy use for cooling if we can maintain continuous shade. It's right here,"—he taps a figure with his pencil—"and if the membranes perform as expected, interior temperatures drop by at least three degrees. That's not even counting the initial investment in cooling systems."

"Three degrees," I repeat, as if the phrase were more than a number. Three degrees less heat. Three degrees more freedom.

Allison nods, writing down notes.

"That's an argument. Carver won't be able to call it 'frills.'"

Suddenly, the room doesn't feel as hostile. The air conditioner still freezes, the projector still hums, the paper clips still lie scattered on my desk. But now the noise has edges: Samuel turns it into data, Allison into discourse, and I into images. For an instant, the three pieces fit together.

"Matt," Samuel says without looking up, still absorbed in his notes. "You're not alone in this."

The words take me by surprise. Samuel isn't one for grand statements. He usually speaks in measurements, percentages, margins of error. Maybe that's why his words carry more weight—they're few, but accurate.

I look at the rendering on the screen. The projected canopies seem to breathe. It looks like our ideas to save the project might actually work. In my eyes, they're still wings; in Samuel's notebook, they're calculations; in Allison's notes, a sales plan. All at once. All necessary.

Allison stays silent for a long moment, then speaks calmly.

"With these changes to the structure and canopy placement, costs will drop enough to absorb the increase in steel and still keep us within budget. Plus,"—she taps the table lightly with her pen— "we still have the same advantage we've repeated over and over: avoiding the investment in cooling systems for the entire plaza. With those figures, we're proving the project can go on exactly as it was conceived. Carver won't have a way to justify cuts that strip away its essence."

I feel my lungs breathing again.

Even so, Travis Patterson's echo keeps haunting me: "This is too complicated, Matt." The phrase hides between papers, beneath the projector light, even behind Samuel's numbers. This time, I don't keep it to myself.

"Today, Travis said this was too complicated," I admit, my voice lower than I expected. "I don't know… that word hits differently. As if he wasn't just talking about the project, but about me."

Samuel lifts his head and sets the pencil aside.

"'Complicated' isn't the same as 'impossible,' Matt. It just means it's worth working through. If it were easy, anyone could do it."

Allison meets my eyes. She doesn't have to do anything to sound firm:

"And besides, Carver and Travis see numbers. You see what's behind them. Sometimes what others call 'complicated' is exactly what makes us necessary—people like you, like Dave, like me."

The words fall like stones on water: they create ripples that spread out and linger. I breathe. It's not that the echo disappears, but for the first time, I'm not hearing it alone.

The conference room is empty after Allison and Samuel leave. The projector shut off with a tired buzz, as if it, too, needed rest. The blueprints remain on the table, covered in pencil marks and notes along the margins.

I return to my office. The paper clips are still there, scattered since morning. I gather them and press them in my hand until I feel the cold metal against my skin. They don't fix anything, but for a moment, they give me the sense that the pieces might come back together.

My phone vibrates. A message from Allison:

"You've got plenty of allies in this. Whatever's missing, we'll figure it out tomorrow. Get some rest."

I stare at the message longer than I need to. Sometimes the most challenging part isn't the work left unfinished, but knowing—really knowing—that someone's there to help carry it.

I don't go straight home. I decide to walk.

Outside, Dallas greets me with its double face: glass towers that look just unveiled, and at their feet, brick buildings that have been holding up entire streets for decades.

The contrast doesn't bother me; it draws me in, as if the city itself understood that beauty doesn't come from choosing one era over another, but from letting time coexist.

I walk slowly, without hurry, without direction. Each step resonates softly against the lines of the pavement—marks that seem to divide the night into manageable fragments. The cool air wraps around me in gentle gusts, not forceful, but like a hand brushing hair back before moving on.

I lift my eyes, and the streetlights line up like a chain of tamed fireflies, guiding my steps. I watch my shoes move forward and notice the precision with which the sidewalks set a rhythm: line, space; line, space. It's as if the city had built a metronome just to remind me that some steps are meant to be taken slowly, without chasing anything.

I breathe. The air smells of warm concrete, distant gasoline, and bread still baking in a small shop somewhere. And for the first time all day, I feel my body and mind moving in sync.

I think that I am also that contrast: the boy who kept drawings in a shoebox under his bed, and the architect who now fights to hold on to canopies against merciless budgets. I can't erase either one. I can only learn to let them stand together.

In one corner, a century-old coffee shop with a façade that reflects the moon as if it were its own. Across the street, a tower casts its green neon onto the damp sidewalk. The contrast makes me smile—each with its own language, yet both saying the same thing: I'm here.

I stop next to a bench. The shadow of a tree draws an arch across the pavement. The orange glow of the streetlights frames it like an invisible urban model. I close my eyes for a moment. The city doesn't demand anything from me. It just offers its mixture, its patience.

And I understand: maybe belonging isn't about being of one time or another, one voice or another. Perhaps it's finding a way to hold all the layers at once, the way this city does.

With that thought, I walk toward the parking lot. The night air feels less cold. The city breathes with me. And in my mind, I can almost hear it—Toby is already waiting, impatient as ever.

Humberto M. Sotomayor

8 Saved Messages

The office smells of reheated coffee and damp paper, slick with the sweat of my hands. It's too late, and the table is still full: blueprints spread open, renderings glowing on the screen, a list of tasks that seems to multiply on its own. Everything is in order—every file is labeled, every meeting is scheduled, and every delivery is marked in the calendar. And yet, time slips through my fingers like water.

The opening is approaching faster than I dare to admit out loud. Everything is on schedule—the steel columns are already in place, the installations are advancing, and the teams are moving in sync. No delays, no errors. The project breathes with the same precision I poured into every blueprint. And still, inside me, pressure beats like a warning—as if the clock were shouting that a thousand things remain undone, that the smallest detail could bring everything down.

Today, for example, the steel delivery arrived three hours late— only three hours. No one on the team saw it as a problem; there was still enough time to move forward. But to me, it felt as if the calendar had mocked me to my face—as if the entire construction had shifted like an inch toward the edge of an abyss. If three hours can slip by, what will happen when it's three days? What if something breaks right before the opening?

I run my hands over my face. The air conditioner whirrs insistently in the corner, colder than usual, as if it were trying to pierce through my skin. My eyes burn with fatigue, but excitement keeps me awake. Whenever I think of the finished building, I'm struck by that impossible mixture: pride that lifts me and anxiety that pulls me under.

Allison scolded me two hours ago. "Go home, Matt. You can't control everything at this hour." She said it in that dry, patient tone when she's done arguing. I nodded on the call, like someone promising something he doesn't intend to keep. I can't leave. Not yet. Not while there are still papers on the table. Not while the thought of an invisible mistake keeps breathing down my neck.

The lamp above the desk casts a white light, falling directly on the blueprints as if interrogating them. I catch myself straightening rulers, aligning folders, erasing smudges along the margins. It isn't just perfectionism; it's the need for everything to be in its place. Because if the papers are out of order, what's to stop the future of the building from being the same?

I lean over a frozen rendering on the screen. The steel skeleton is taking shape. I see it in digital colors but feel it as something alive—bones waiting for skin, a body that still needs to hold itself up to live. It thrills me as much as it terrifies me.

I move a folder to make space, and something slips to the floor. I bend to pick it up: a napkin, folded in quarters, yellowed at the edges, with the faded logo of a New Orleans hotel. I bring it closer: it smells of old paper and stale coffee; the fiber is rough, crackling faintly as I unfold it.

The blue ink has faded, but it can still be read:

"Matty, I'm always so proud of you, and today I'm happy to be part of your dreams.
Your Ellie."

The air conditioner keeps humming, but I no longer hear it. I feel the brush of paper against my fingers—the rough texture of an ordinary napkin that, for some reason, has managed to survive everything.

A knot tightens in my throat, which seems like it won't let me speak, and my eyes grow slightly glassy. I remember her laughter as she wrote it. She always left me notes on whatever scrap of paper was at hand—some with our inside jokes, all full of affection and honesty. That careless habit of using the first thing she could find to leave me a message that wasn't a joke, even when it came wrapped in one.

She was the first person I ever showed all my dreams to. And the first to say they were hers, too.

I close my eyes. The office disappears.

The car engine is running, but we haven't pulled out yet. I've spent the last two hours ensuring everything is in order: suitcases in the trunk, arranged by weight and size; the tank full; water bottles lined up in the center compartment. The hotel reservation—printed and sealed in a plastic folder—rests between the seat and the console. Everything ready. Everything under control.

That's how my mind works: nothing should go off course if the route is planned.

On the other hand, Elena comes running out of the house with a suitcase that looks like it's about to burst. The zipper is half open, a sweater sticking out like a tongue of fabric ready to esca-

pe. In her other hand, she's holding a pair of shoes she forgot to pack. She laughs to herself, as if her own disorder were a private joke.

"Matty, don't worry about the time—there's no rush on this trip," she says, almost singing, while tossing the suitcase into the trunk without checking how I've arranged the others.

I take a deep breath. The space had been perfectly measured, and now fabric spills like an ungovernable obstacle. I want to tell her to zip it properly and fold things neatly, reminding her that a loose bag makes noise and makes the ride longer. But she looks so happy, that smile bright enough to soften the gray morning, that I bite my tongue. I simply adjust things as needed and close the trunk. She flashes me a triumphant wink, as if she knows she's won a small, invisible battle.

We get in the car. Elena takes a minute to buckle her seatbelt—she got the strap tangled up with her handbag. She laughs out loud and glances sideways at me.

"If you can survive traveling with me, you can survive anything."

I don't answer. I tighten my grip on the steering wheel and check the mirrors. She reaches out and turns on the stereo. Classic country floods the cabin—plain guitars, rough voices. She starts singing even though she doesn't know all the lyrics. She makes up the parts she doesn't know, trades lyrics for rhymed syllables, and drums the dashboard with her palm like a makeshift percussionist. The music wraps around her; it passes through me differently. I hear the silences between chords, the steady cadence that repeats like a faithful metronome.

"Come on, Matty!" she insists. "Take the harmony."

"I don't know the lyrics."

"Neither do I!" she laughs again, that clear laughter brightening any space it touches.

The road hasn't even begun, but I know this trip won't follow my lists. And at the same time, I find myself starting to smile, which I didn't expect.

She runs back into the house because she's forgotten her jacket. I sigh in protest, but I don't start the car. I watch her cross the yard again like a child with no sense of time. Her hair flies wildly, her voice is heard from the door: "I'll be right back, Matty!" When she returns, she's holding the jacket, an open pack of cookies, and the unshakable belief that being ten minutes late doesn't matter.

In my mind, ten minutes means a lot. It's ten lines in the agenda, a margin that can throw off the schedule for the next gas stop. But when she hands me a cookie without asking and says, "Come on, try it," the calculation starts to fall apart. The sweet taste, mixed with the echo of her laughter, forces me to admit there are things you can't measure in minutes or maps.

We finally pull out. The engine vibrates under my hands like a promise. I look in the rearview mirror—the house recedes, the itinerary begins. Elena turns up the volume on the stereo and props her feet on the dashboard, even after I tell her it's not safe. She answers with another laugh and a light shrug, as if to say, "Relax, Matty, not everything has to be perfect."

The road opens ahead of us. I think about the miles to go, the hotels where we'll sleep, and the restaurants I've marked as "safe options." On the other hand, she already imagines stopping at any gas station for candy or pulling into any diner for a hot dog. And I know it because she says it out loud, as if there were no line between thinking and speaking.

"Let's stop wherever we feel like it," she declares. "And I want one of those cheap coffees that taste like plastic, you hear me, Matty?"

I don't say anything. I keep my eyes on the road. But deep down, I'm smiling again. I know that no matter how hard I try to resist, that will be the real map of this trip—her improvising, and *me trying not to lose control.*

There's already some traffic on the outskirts of the city. The traffic lights seem to last longer than they should, and every minute weighs on my mind like a reminder of how fragile any itinerary can be. Elena, meanwhile, sings without a care, as if time were an unnecessary invention. I hold back the urge to point out the hour. It's five hundred miles to New Orleans, and I made myself a promise: to let go, have fun, enjoy Elena, and the time we have together. Even if it kills me, I'll try.

The highway stretches out like an infinite line. Two lanes seem to get lost in the horizon, flat fields on either side, power poles keeping rhythm like metronomes nailed to the earth. The sun isn't burning yet, but hints at the dry heat that will settle by noon. The steering wheel starts to feel warm under my palms; a mosquito hits the windshield, leaving a dark streak that annoys me more than it should. The air smells of hot asphalt mixed with old gasoline drifting from some distant truck. I keep my hands steady on the wheel, holding a perfect speed: seventy miles an hour, not one more or less.

Elena keeps her window cracked—though I prefer them closed with the air conditioning on, I don't say anything—and lets the wind tangle her hair. She sings along to the music as if she were on stage. She has that gift for turning any space into an impromptu concert, for finding joy in any moment, even inside the most worn-out car on the highway.

Country music drifts through the speakers—simple lyrics about trains, highways, and broken hearts. She doesn't know half the lyrics, but that doesn't matter; she makes up sounds, changes lines, slips my name into the middle of a verse as if the song were written for us.

"▯ Matty drives too seriously, Matty counts the miles... ▯" she sings, mimicking the singer's rough voice before bursting into lau-

ghter that fills the whole car.

I try to keep a straight face, but my mouth betrays me into a smile. She grabs the seatbelt and strums it like a guitar string. Occasionally, she glances my way, searching for the crack in my concentration. She knows she's found it when my hands tap the steering wheel in time with the song.

The first gas station appears in the middle of nowhere. I pull in because it was part of the plan—half a tank, time to refuel, and clean the windshield before moving on. The midday heat sticks to my back as I pump the gas.

Ellie's already disappeared into the store. When I follow, I find her at the counter with an absurd haul: a giant bag of chips, a cheap cowboy hat with red feathers, a box of doughnuts, and a lot of candies that barely fit in her arms.

"What do we need all that for?" I ask, raising an eyebrow.

"To survive, Matty. Or did your itinerary account for sudden hunger attacks?" she says with mock seriousness before breaking into another laugh.

"At least tell me you got water," I say, eyeing the pile of junk like evidence from a crime scene.

"Water?" she fakes surprise. "Why would we need water on a road trip? Dr Pepper and Coke will make it way more fun."

She shakes the bottles like trophies and gives me a wink. I take a slow breath, reminding myself of my promise to let go. Even so, in my head, I'm already calculating how many grams of sugar are in each bottle.

The cashier watches us with amusement as he scans each item. Ellie takes the opportunity to drop a glow-in-the-dark rubber ball on the counter.

"This too. You never know when you'll need a radioactive toy in the middle of Texas."

I shake my head, but pay anyway. On the way out, she puts on the ridiculous cowboy hat and, without asking, stuffs a doughnut directly into my mouth with a triumphant grin. I chew in silence, pretending to be annoyed, though inside I smile.

"See? We're already on vacation."

The sugar clings to my tongue back in the car, but I still take another bite. She licks the crumbs from her fingers, then turns up the music. Another country song comes on, the chorus repeating over and over about coming home. She shouts the lyrics as if she were on stage. I focus on the shadows cast by the power poles across the asphalt—a dark line slides over the windshield every ten seconds. One, two, three, four... I count them as if that might somehow keep time under control.

"What are you counting now?" she asks, still singing along.

"Power poles. The rhythm they appear in," I answer without thinking.

"Matty, do you realize you're counting shadows?"

"Someone has to."

"No, honey," she laughs, brushing my arm lightly. "No one has to. Just you. And I love that."

She says it tenderly, without teasing. For a second, I stop counting. The landscape keeps moving anyway, untouched by my attention, and nothing happens.

A few miles later, an old motel appears, its rusted sign promising "Pool & Wi-Fi" in faded red letters. Ellie wants to stop just to see if the pool still exists. I keep driving, straight along the line of the plan. She sighs dramatically—but five minutes later, she's laughing again, this time at a passing truck painted with a grinning cow.

"Look, Matty—it's your twin!" she says, pointing at the ridiculous drawing.

I don't get the joke, but her laughter is contagious anyway. The trip goes on. The sun climbs higher. The highway stretches *into an endless thread between sky and earth, and I think it doesn't matter if the destination comes late, as long as she keeps singing beside me.*

The gray ribbon of road seems endless—until a red flicker breaks the monotony of the horizon: a blinking sign promising coffee and shade.

The neon sign flickers like an eye too weary to stay open.

«DINER».

Below it, a red arrow points toward a metal door that's been painted so many times, no one knows its original color. The parking lot is nearly complete: dust-covered pickups, faded chrome motorcycles, and cars from other decades that look like they've repeatedly made this same trip to this very spot. With that many vehicles, I figure the food must be good.

I park beside an old gas pump—more decorative than functional; the heat radiating from the metal makes the air thick and shimmering. Ellie steps out wearing her ridiculous hat and lets out a triumphant whistle, as if she's just discovered buried treasure in the middle of the highway.

As we enter, country music spills from a jukebox in the corner. The air conditioning drops like instant relief, starkly contrasting to the dry heat that's followed us here. The smell is homey: freshly fried food, grilled meat with spices, and a hint of barbecue that permeates the walls.

Everyone inside looks local, carrying that easy, unhurried joy you can read straight off their smiles. The floor is old wood, worn smooth but clean; every step creaks like we've stepped into a cowboy movie. Rodeo photos, leather trinkets, horseshoes, and neon signs hang across the walls. Everything's cluttered, almost chaotic, yet it holds together with perfect balance—the kind of order that belongs to a place that knows exactly what it is.

"This is perfect," Ellie says, as if the word had been made for places like this.

We sit by the window. The glass is a little greasy on the inside and streaked by old rain on the outside. A waitress with a pencil behind her ear and red-painted nails greets us with a casual smile.

"What'll it be, hon?" she asks me, but Ellie already has her hand up.

"Two coffees, please. His black"—she points my way—"and mine with way too much sugar. And..." she scans the menu, eyes lighting up, "a slice of apple pie the size of Texas."

"We have 'highway size' and 'storm size,'" the waitress says with a wink.

"'Storm,' obviously," Ellie replies, delighted. "And add ice cream on top if the universe allows it."

I open the menu to hide my embarrassment—grainy photos of impossible burgers, eternal eggs, milkshakes that defy physics. I'll stick with coffee, nothing more. Ellie looks at me as if I've just failed some invisible contest.

"Matty, don't marry your coffee. Look—this pie comes with the promise of saving musical souls."

"It doesn't say that," I answer, pointing to a line that only mentions cinnamon.

"It says so in spirit," she laughs. "Besides, today we're tourists of the present. Anything goes."

The coffees arrive in thick mugs, the glaze marked by tiny cracks. Mine tastes like a long drive at night; Ellie's like a sugary carnival. She blows on hers, as if chasing ghosts from the steam.

When the pie arrives, the plate lands with a soft thud. The slice glistens under a coat of syrup; the crust looks like a cracked map. The ice cream melts down the sides, forming pale rivers that disappear into the apple.

"Just one bite," she says, cutting me off before I can object. "Just one. If you don't like it, I'll make the heroic sacrifice of finishing it myself."

I hold her gaze for a moment. She picks up the fork, cuts a precise corner, blows on it, and holds it out to me as if training a wild animal. I think about the itinerary, the minutes, the gas, sugar, and the invisible rules that have often kept me safe.

I open my mouth. The first bite is warm cinnamon, pie crust, and soft apple bursting with pure sweetness. I say nothing. She understood the silence and offered me another, smaller piece, claiming victory without making a scene.

"See?" she whispers. "Even the plan can move with us."

Across the counter, a man in a cowboy hat talks with the waitress as if they were family. Two truckers argue about a high school score I've never heard of. An elderly couple shares a milkshake with two straws. Everything seems to have its own rhythm, independent of clocks. Outside, the sky begins to wrinkle into a dull gray. The first raindrops hit the tin roof like a handful of marbles thrown from above.

"Storm-size storm," Ellie says, delighted with her own order. She stands and presses her forehead to the glass. "Look, Matty— the road's improvising too."

The raindrops swell, collide, and race down the window as if competing. Behind us, the waitress turns up the jukebox just a little—soft jazz now: a worn-out sax, a shy piano, a drum set that speaks in whispers. Ellie sits back down with the smile of someone who's just discovered a secret.

"I like it when the world decides the tempo," she says. "Not you, not me. The world."

I cradle my cup in both hands. The warmth runs through my fingers and up my wrist. I want to hurry, pay the bill, and get back on the road before the pavement turns slick. I know because I make a mental note of it. But then I see her laughing, her forehead fogging from the glass, and something in me loosens. There's logic in her disorder, measure in her excess. The music seems to underscore it: it's not rushing, it's not arriving, it just exists.

"Can I ask you something strange?" she says suddenly, staring at the pie as if it were an oracle.

"Always."

"How long does it take to get somewhere when you're already thinking about the next place?"

I don't answer. She squeezes my fingers across the table—a brief pressure, like checking a pulse.

"I'm not asking you to change," she whispers. "Just to let me sit with you on the map. Here. Now."

The rain grows heavier for a minute, then fades into slow diagonals. The puddles outside catch the neon light and turn it into chunks of red fruit. The waitress leaves an extra napkin, and Ellie takes it to draw a crooked heart with the pen she carries in her bag. Beneath it, she writes "Stop counting, start tasting" and slides it to me like she's signing an armistice. I don't sign, but fold it carefully and tuck it into my shirt pocket. She watches me, pleased.

We pay. As I walk toward the door, I turn back for one last look at this unique place. Outside, the air smells of wet earth—a scent that lasts only as long as a summer rain. The asphalt gleams like a mirror, and I can feel the faint vibration of distant trucks passing by under my feet.

"Come on," Ellie says, stretching her hand to me. "Let's go before the road gets jealous."

In the car, the windshield still carries a few stubborn drops. I turn on the wipers; their hypnotic swing clears thin stripes for a second before the blur returns. I drive slowly. She props her bare feet on the seat, gazing out the window as if every puddle were a *planet. She turns up the music—now a singer dragging her vowels like long-tailed comets.*

"You know what I like about you?" she asks, still looking at what's left of the rain.

"Should I be worried?"

"That you try to hold the world still so it doesn't crash down on me. And sometimes, it works." She laughs. "But today, it's your turn to let the world move. I'll hold on tight."

I smile. I don't answer. The windshield wipers keep their rhythm—a rhythm I didn't set. I slow down a bit and take her hand. Along the roadside, puddles reflect the poles like musical notes. I think about all that's left to build, and all that already stands without my permission. Ellie starts singing again, softly, almost to herself. I listen, and for a moment, I don't count anything. I just drive. The road continues, the rain finally surrenders, and in my mind, an invisible line connects the apple pie, the red neon, and the silent promise to keep learning to be present.

We walk hand in hand down Bourbon Street at night, when it turns pedestrian and stops being a street to become a human river. The air is thick, humid, almost liquid; every breath carries traces of spilled beer, Cajun spices, and sweet tobacco. The iron balconies seem to sweat with colorful lights, like flags hanging as an extension of skin.

The street vibrates with music from every direction—trumpets bursting from a bar, a lone saxophone on the corner, drums pounding improvised rhythms on the pavement. Everything blends into a chaotic harmony that somehow sounds like music. Here, everything seems to exist for celebration and joy.

Ellie smiles as if she's been here in another life. She squeezes my hand and pulls me into the middle of the crowd. I try to keep up, but every detail distracts me—the geometry of the balconies, the broken symmetry of the lamp posts, the reflection of neon on wet cobblestones. She lives the music; I calculate the shadow a streetlight casts across the stones.

"Matty," she says, turning slightly to look at me, "you're here, right? With me."

"Of course," I answer, though my voice is lost in the sound of a discordant trumpet.

She laughs, eyes locking onto mine, as if she's just uncovered my distraction.

"Tell me the truth... are you seeing buildings or breathing?"

I don't know how to answer. Because I'm doing both—breathing geometries, measuring shadows, and studying proportions as if they were oxygen. And yet, I hear her, feel her close. Her laughter forces me to loosen, just a little, the invisible measurements I carry inside.

With a tug of her hand, she pulls me into a tiny bar where a quartet plays jazz as if their lives depended on it. The saxophone cries long notes, the trumpet answers in short bursts, the piano glides like a slow river, and the drums hold everything together with gentle beats. The walls sweat dampness and yellow light; the sticky floor creaks under every step. Ellie orders two glasses of cheap wine and raises hers as if toasting to something secret.

"To you, Matty. To this trip."

I sip slowly. The wine tastes like iron and overripe fruit, but the way she lifts her glass turns it into something different—a ritual of belonging. She smiles, lips stained red, and takes a photo of me with an instant camera she pulled out of nowhere. The flash blinds me for a second. She shakes the photo, waits for the image to appear, then tucks it away like treasure.

"There," she says. "Now you're really here."

We leave the bar and continue walking down Bourbon Street—bars everywhere, balconies crowded with people throwing colored necklaces, musicians improvising on the sidewalks. Everything feels like too much, and yet somehow perfect.

I follow her lead. She moves through the crowd as if the city were hers. On the other hand, I keep counting windows, measuring balconies, and tracing the proportions of the arches. But this time, I do it without letting go of her hand.

We slip into two more bars without meaning to. The first is small, dimly lit—the jazz here is soft, intimate: a bass beating like a tired heart, a piano that caresses more than it plays, and a rough voice that sounds like it's lived a thousand lives. Ellie leans against the bar, eyes closed, nodding to the rhythm, half-signing along as if the song had been written for her. I watch the light ripple through her hair, the smoke floating in layers, the dark wood creaking beneath our feet.

The second bar is the opposite: electric blues, roaring guitars, clapping hands keeping time, a drummer sweating beneath the neon. People sing, dance, stomp their boots against the floor, and Ellie dives into the wave like someone fluent in its language. I follow—awkwardly—but she grabs my shoulders, spins me just enough, and laughs as if it doesn't matter that my steps don't match the beat.

"See, Matty?" she shouts into my ear, between the guitars and the laughter. "No reservations, no schedules, no clocks. You just walk in and enjoy the music wherever you land. That's all."

I nod, though I'm still counting chords in my head, as if searching for a hidden pattern. But when I see her jumping and laughing, I realize maybe there's nothing to find. Perhaps it's enough just to be.

Outside, the street throbs even louder. We pass a massive

143

casino that looks as if it's been airlifted straight from Rome, with pillars like the Parthenon's. Ellie stops.

"Five minutes. I swear, no more," she says.

Before I can say a word, she's already inside. I catch up to her in the entrance, and she grabs my hand, pulling me eagerly through the doors. We walk through endless rows of slot machines blinking like neon constellations—green, red, violet lights; electronic sounds colliding in a language impossible to decipher.

Ellie's wearing the colored-bead necklaces we bought at a souvenir shop just for fun, and with every step, she seems to shine brighter. Her warm skin catches the casino's light and softens it, as if the whole city were reflected in her. Her beauty is natural, but what really draws every eye is her joy—the way she gives herself to the moment, as if nothing else existed.

I let myself go and follow her lead. She sits at one machine, then another, playing just a few rounds at each, laughing even as we lose a couple of dollars in seconds. Money doesn't seem to matter to her; what's fun is the game itself, the feeling of improvising.

Finally, we reach a corner where the machines look like relics from another age—stubborn buttons, faded colors on the screens, survivors of generations of players. Ellie folds her arms and looks at me with mock solemnity.

"Pick one, Matty," she says, narrowing her eyes like a fortune-teller from New Orleans. "I can feel it—luck's hiding right here."

I smile, skeptical, but point at one at random. She claps like she's uncovered a fate written in the cards. She inserts a crumpled bill and hits the button. Three figures spin, stop with an absurd clink... and the screen announces a ¡Jackpot—$500!

Ellie screams like she's won the lottery, throws her arms around me, and kisses me, laughing loud enough to turn heads.

"See, Matty?! Even luck's telling you to have fun with me!"

The night rolled on in laughter, drinks, and games. We wandered from one place to another, tried our luck at more machines, and toasted with strangers who felt like old friends. I—who always want everything under control—ended up swept away by her joy like a current impossible to resist. That night was pure celebration: lights, music, noise, and laughter—one of those nights that, even when memory fades, stays etched in you forever.

The following night, the restaurant greets us with quiet formality. At the entrance, the hostess—elegant and composed—checks the reservation list with a practiced, yet genuine smile.

"Mr. Prescott, your table is ready."

I nod silently, feeling that familiar mix of pride and discomfort that comes from hearing my own name spoken by someone else—as if it belonged to me, and yet somehow did not.

Ellie squeezes my hand, and we walk a few steps forward. The first thing I see is the bar—broad, glowing under a central chandelier that scatters light across a parade of bottles lined up like liquid-stained glass. For a moment, I think of stopping there, but tonight I'm with someone unique, someone special.

Beyond it, the dining room opens with quiet solemnity: high walls of dark wood, angled mirrors catching golden flashes, sconces pouring their light like a gentle touch over the white tablecloths. The air hums with low voices and discreet jazz, a rhythm that seems to invite you to let your guard down. The hostess leads us to the corner. The most secluded table—the most romantic one— waits beneath a soft lamp that casts an intimate circle of light within the vast hall.

We sit down. The leather chair yields beneath my weight, and

I feel the cold texture of the perfectly aligned silverware. Ellie smiles as if the place belonged to her, as if the whole setting had been arranged for her alone.

"Look, Matty," she whispers, "even the glasses seem to dance with the light."

She orders a juicy steak with au gratin potatoes. I choose the same, caring more about the way she describes it than about the food. The wine arrives—dark, poured with ceremony. We toast. She clinks her glass against mine with a gesture that seems to say: we're here, right now.

We start our conversation talking about small things—the trip, the music on Bourbon Street, the brief storm the afternoon before. But slowly, between sips of wine and unhurried bites, something in me opens. The table turns into a space for confession.

"Do you want to know what I really dream of?" I ask, almost without thinking.

She sets her glass down and looks at me, attentive, as if she'd been waiting for that question all along.

I spoke then, my words unfolding like a confession. I talk to her about the building I've been imagining for years—a space that breathes, one that isn't limited to holding offices but embraces the people who inhabit it. I talk to her about the light that spills in like a gentle greeting, the water that quiets the noise, the materials that speak the truth of what they are. I talk about belonging—about how a place can teach you to feel that you belong to something greater than yourself.

I confess it's more than a project. It's the only language I know—the way I've learned to express myself. It's what I hope to leave behind: proof that a space can make anyone—whether loud or quiet—feel they belong.

I pause without meaning to. The jazz keeps playing in the background—the bass pulsing softly, the piano tracing loose notes, as if the music itself were keeping pace with my voice. It surprises me how everything aligns—my hesitant words, that quiet rhythm—as though the whole room were holding up my confession.

I tell her this building is a dream that's followed me for as long as I can remember—older than any blueprint, deeper than any rendering. What matters isn't the glass, or the steel, or even the wood, but the silent promise I made as a child: to prove that a place could embrace everyone.

When I finish, she keeps looking at me. No interruption, no easy smile—just that steady, deep gaze that seems to hold me together.

"Matty..." she says at last, her voice slightly trembling. "You have no idea how happy it makes me that you're showing me this. That you're letting me in."

I lower my eyes, uneasy, but she leans forward, takes my hand on the table, and squeezes it tightly.

"I'm always proud of you," she says. "But now... now I feel like you're making me part of something bigger than the two of us."

I don't know what to answer. I only nod, swallowing a knot that even the wine can't dissolve.

Later that night, in the hotel room, the formality of the restaurant gives way to play. Ellie first takes off her golden necklace, still gleaming against her slender neck, and sets it gently on the table. Then, one by one, she arranges the colorful beads left over from the day before, now souvenirs of a distant celebration. Her elegant dress slips away with natural ease, replaced by a soft pajama that feels made for another kind of night—more intimate, slower, as romantic as the dinner we've just shared.

147

She lies back on the bed, laughing, but her laughter isn't the loud one from the street anymore; now it's a whisper that lights up the room without dazzling it.

She reaches gently toward the nightstand to grab her purse and pulls out a pen. Then she takes the first thing within reach—a hotel napkin. Sitting on the edge of the bed, she writes quickly, folding the napkin as if tucking away a secret.

"All done," she says, handing it to me with a solemn gesture and bright eyes.

I unfold it. The blue ink still glistens, wet:

"Matty, I am always so proud of you, and tonight I am happy that you have made me part of your dreams.
Your Ellie."

I sit there in silence—the napkin held between my hands. Its rough paper grazes my skin, yet what I feel is tenderness—an unfamiliar warmth spreading through my chest. She watches me, waiting for a reaction, yet all I can do is pull her close, holding her as if the whole world could fit inside that embrace.

The napkin remains folded on the nightstand beneath the soft glow of the lamp that seems to frame it. Ellie settles beside me, her steady breathing rocking the air like a lullaby. I turn off the light and close my eyes, knowing that small piece of paper will forever keep what I couldn't say aloud.

That night, there were no blueprints, no calculations— only the quiet certainty that, for once, someone saw me and loved me completely, without expecting anything in return.

The air conditioner buzzes again in my office. I open my eyes—no jazz, no beads, no Ellie laughing on a hotel bed. Only the pale glow of the paused screen and the napkin in my hands, more fragile than I remembered, yet still intact. The hotel logo is almost gone; the blue ink has faded around the edges, but the words remain stubborn, as if refusing to yield to time.

I take a slow breath. I think of everything I've lost, of everything I failed to hold together. But also think about this: that not everything was lost. There were nights when I didn't count windows or review calculations, when I simply was present. And though it feels distant now, it still exists within me.

I fold the napkin carefully, as if it were a fragile relic holding more life than it appears to, and place it inside a desk drawer. The sound of it closing is brief and definitive—a silent pact with memory.

I sit for a moment, staring at the empty desk surface, feeling the urge to write, to put into words what still beats inside me. My notebook is at home, waiting for me as always, but I don't want to wait. I take a blank sheet of paper from the printer, set it before me, and begin to write slowly, as if each line needed to breathe:

> *"Today I understood that I've had many happy moments. Not all of them stayed with me, but some are still here. And that's enough to know it was all worth it."*

I fold the page with the same care I gave the napkin. I slip this one into my shirt pocket to take home, where it will find its rightful place in the notebook that keeps all my memories.

I rest my forehead in my hands for a moment. The murmur of the office fills the air again. But something inside me has quieted: I know there are still pieces of my life no one can take away.

I look up. The desk lamp is still on, the computer screen asleep, as if time itself had passed in silence. I don't know how long I was lost in the memory; I only see that night has settled outside. I slowly stand up, grab my keys, and turn off the lights. It's time to go home. Toby is waiting for me. And finally, I need to rest too.

9 At the Edge

"My anxiety doesn't come from thinking about the future,
but from wanting to control it."
— **Hugh Prather, *Notes to Myself***

The morning sun blazes down on the steel beams, its radiant glare shattering into a thousand sparks that make me squint. The air carries the rough blend of dust, wet concrete, and the crew's sweat. With every step, the gravel crunches beneath my boots, steady and dry, while the sounds of the site fold over one another relentlessly— the pound of a jackhammer, distant shouts of command, the groan of a crane turning in slow, almost choreographed motion.

I pace slowly along the perimeter of the construction site, white helmet on, iPad in hand, blueprints under my arm. It's been two weeks since my last visit, but every time I come, it demands my full attention. Here, nothing can be left to chance: every joint, every angle, every measurement has to be exact. And even though I trust my team, I can't shake the feeling that if I don't see it with my own eyes, something might slip off track without anyone noticing.

The engineers surround me with their technical updates:

—"The north wing foundation's ready to pour by Friday."

—"We're fine-tuning the electrical installations; the supplier says delivery is tomorrow."

—"The main elevator is already in testing."

I nod, ask questions, and jot notes in the margins of the blueprints. Sometimes I don't answer right away; I just stand still, watching a single point—a column, a weld, a hanging cable—as if that one detail might hold the answer to everything.

The crew seems grateful that I'm here. I can tell by their gestures—a firmer handshake than usual, the way they call me "architect" with a respect that feels genuine. I know my presence tells them their work matters, that someone is linking the small pieces to the larger dream.

I climb the metal stairs, still lacking railings. Each step trembles slightly under my weight, releasing a dry, metallic creak. I hold the clipboard of blueprints tight against my chest, like a shield. Reaching the second level, I pause.

From here, the building's skeleton opens into corridors of gray concrete. They're still only bare walls—doorways waiting for frames, windows without glass—but in my mind, they're already alive. I see the hallway bathed in morning light, people walking in with folders under their arms, exchanging hurried greetings. I see the open rooms, daylight falling in clean diagonals I drew months ago. The present dust transforms, in my imagination, into crisp air filtered through shadows.

I walk more slowly, letting the spaces speak. Every line, every opening, every wall seems to whisper: I'm here. Just bones, but here.

I climb to the third floor. The air feels heavier here, as if the sun had trapped its heat between the unfinished walls. From this vantage point, I can see the city unfolding in the distance—traffic flowing like a far-off river, neighboring buildings flashing shards of glass. I lean against a steel frame and close my eyes for a moment. I imagined this same angle years ago, in a rendering that felt like an impossible dream. Now it's here—unfinished, but alive.

I walk along what will soon be the line of offices. Where there's dust and echo now, I hear hurried footsteps, overlapping voices, the faint buzz of computers. Where there's rough concrete, I picture glass filtering the afternoon light without glare. Where there are scaffolds, I see vines climbing the walls, soft shadows softening the edges.

I don't speak. I just walk. It feels as though the building is breathing with me—each floor higher, each staircase a new pulse. Sometimes I run my hand along the concrete, the roughness that will soon turn smooth. Other times, I look up, following the steel beams as they stretch into the bright air.

It's my dream taking shape, piece by piece. And at the same time, it's a creature growing faster than I can hold.

I reach the rooftop. The wind hits harder up here, thick with dust and the smell of welding. No railings yet—only slabs of concrete and steel leaning toward the open air. From this height, the building seems to hover over the city. The horizon spreads wide, the avenues stretch like veins, the sun glints off faraway towers. Everything is half-finished, and yet it carries a kind of greatness—a skeleton already promising the skin it will wear.

I stand still for a few seconds. Eyes closed, the noise of drills and hammers shifts into what I imagine: footsteps, voices, the background noise of a living place. I think that someday, someone will stop up here—someone who'll never know my name—and look out at the city with the same quiet sense of belonging. That thought hits me and strengthens me all at once.

I head back down, enjoying the walk, feeling as if the place were already real—functional, full of people. I make my way to the central courtyard that will soon become the lobby. Here the noise returns, multiplied: the shouts of the crew, the rumble of concrete being

153

poured, the rhythmic clang of rebar being aligned. I step carefully between piles of gravel and temporary scaffolding, watching where I place my feet.

A young engineer walks beside me, explaining something about the main slab.

"If we can pour this section before Friday, the rest of the levels will stay on schedule," he says, pointing with his clipboard.

I listen closely, nod, and ask about the most minor details—the concrete strength, curing times, drying periods. Meanwhile, I watch how the light slants in from above, spreading across the gravel floor like an open fan. In my head, it's no longer just an empty courtyard—it's a lobby alive with voices, water running down a wall, footsteps echoing on marble.

I follow the line of the central courtyard, walking through it as if it were already open to the public. But what stands before me is still a raw construction site: bare walls with their steel bones exposed, formwork stacked to one side, cable trays held together with temporary wire, air ducts sealed with black plastic, red and blue pipes jutting out like veins without skin. The floor is a slab of rough concrete, marked by hairline cracks, waiting for marble. Here and there, spray-painted signs mark levels, axes, cuts. Beneath the skylight—still just an empty frame—the light falls in a perfect rectangle across the gravel, like a rehearsal for the shadows that will one day soften the lobby's temperature.

I stop where the reflecting pool will be. For now, it's just a raw concrete box—no finish, no coating, the inspection hatch open, the piping exposed. I crouch and run my hand along the edge: rough, porous, waiting for stone. In my head, I can already hear the sound of water sliding over it; in reality, only the concrete vibrator buzzes from the far corner. To one side, the future reception area is nothing more than a break in the wall, with a temporary board and a plumb line hanging. I picture the marble cladding, the wooden reception desk—simple, unpretending—and the cool breath of the HVAC pushing the heat upward.

I keep walking; my mind doesn't rest. I mentally review the sequence: slab pour—minimum seven days of curing—then patching, polishing, fine leveling, and flooring installation. Deadlines. The skylight glass is in production; any delay in tempering will cost us 3 days. The lobby lights must be tested before the final coating, or we'll ruin the finish. The mechanical trunks look clean, but if the main tray isn't left clear for maintenance, we'll have a headache in two years—potential delays.

An engineer walks over with the mechanical blueprints pulled up on his tablet.

"Architect, the main air unit for the lobby arrives Monday. If we approve the support today, they can fabricate tomorrow and be installed on Friday."

I nod and point to the open space.

"I want the support hidden inside the plinth. Check the height—I need thirteen feet, nine inches clear finished height. And make sure the linear grille doesn't line up with the floor joint; I'd rather break the modulation above than below."

"Got it," he says, already taking notes.

I keep going. On the west side, the curtain wall is little more than a metal frame with exposed insulation. I picture it as a low-emissivity glass surface, filtering the afternoon sun. But my mind is already with the supplier—delivery schedules, hardware calibration, and tolerances. If the structural sealant doesn't cure on schedule, we lose half a week. If the marble arrives with the wrong thickness, we'll have to rework the pieces, and the baseboard layout will fall

155

apart. Deadlines, deadlines. A supervisor nods at me; I return the gesture and ask him to protect the wheelbarrow path with plywood where the stone will go. I don't want any damaged edges anywhere.

I lean over the stairwell opening. It's a concrete spiral with rough steps. In my mind, it already wears a warm wooden skin and a line of light running beneath each tread, like a discreet guide. I jot in my iPad: "check light uniformity—no hot spots." And right away, the next thought comes to mind: DALI control, preset scenes, night tests. Will one night be enough? Two? Add a week's buffer... and what if we lose it all in testing?

I stop beneath the upper opening—the light streams in obliquely and fans across the gravel floor. For a moment, future and present overlap: I hear voices echoing, the soft lapping of water against stone; I feel the coolness of clean air moving gently; I see shadows drawn on the polished floor like a musical score. I blink, and the construction site returns—dust hanging in the air, a cart full of concrete bags, the hollow thud of a falling bucket. And again, without meaning to, my mind jumps ahead: deliveries, testing, patching, hardware, joints, lists, checklist.

"Architect," an installer calls from a scaffold, "does the main conduit for the lobby run up through here, or do you want it along the perimeter?"

"Perimeter," I answer. "And leave an access hatch behind the ceiling panel. I don't want anything broken later if a section ever needs replacing."

I keep walking the site, slower this time, as if each step could somehow screw time in my favor. I know the team is confident, and I know we're still on schedule. But inside, another voice keeps counting what could go wrong. I check my watch. Time's running out. The dream is taking shape before my eyes, floor by floor, and yet it feels like it's growing faster than I can hold it. The construction site keeps its concert of hammers and cranes. I walk, observe, and take notes.

And without saying it aloud, I begin to feel the tension tighten inside me.

Sweat runs down my forehead. I take a deep breath, but it does little to calm me. And, as in college—back when something beyond my control could break—, the world feels like it's crashing down around me.

The wall clock read 8:15 when I walked through the door of the design studio, blueprint under my arm. It was still warm, fresh from the printer; the scent of fresh ink mingled with the cold coffee I carried in my other hand. I rushed to the submission table, but the line had already closed.

The murmur of the others stopped just long enough for me to feel every stare on the back of my neck—quick whispers, a stifled laugh, that thick kind of silence that's louder than noise. My skin burned, as if all those eyes were lamps turned directly on me. The blueprint, stiff and heavy, began to double its weight in my sweaty hands. I wanted to move forward, but it felt like walking through a glass hallway, with everyone watching my every step.

I caught my reflection in the window: wrinkled shirt, sweat-stained collar, deep circles under my eyes from three sleepless nights. Graphite-stained fingers had left dark smudges on the white paper—proof of exhaustion, not carelessness. I'd killed myself perfecting every line, every angle, checking the scale over and over. And yet, none of it mattered: the print shop was half an hour late, and everything fell apart.

The professor—a tall man with square glasses and a voice that never raised its volume—looked at me over the rim of his lenses.

He didn't yell, didn't argue. He just said, in that quiet tone that weighs more than any shout,

"Architecture doesn't forgive excuses."

Those words dropped like a block of concrete. I felt the blood rush to my face. I tightened my lips to keep them from trembling. My eyes searched for a place to look without being seen, but there was nowhere—only rows of classmates pretending not to notice, or watching me with that uneasy glint in their eyes. The paper of my blueprint crackled between my fingers, as if it, too, resented being there, ignored.

The hum of the lights sharpened and grew high-pitched; distant voices blended into a stinging murmur. Even the thud of my heartbeat sounded louder than everything else. I was invisible, and at the same time, exposed at the center of a scene I couldn't stop.

The professor flipped through my late submission, furrowed, then looked up. I remember his words perfectly:

"It's an excellent project, Prescott. Impeccably done. But the rules are clear—the deadline was eight o'clock."

He said it without cruelty, almost with regret, and yet the zero scribbled on the sheet stung more than any reprimand. The entire semester had revolved around that project: hours of research in the library, hand-drawn lines until the paper turned gray from erasing, models made at dawn with the smell of glue. Every line had been weighed and refined, cared for, and yet it all came crashing down because the print shop didn't keep its word.

I remember the exact feeling of helplessness: the line at the counter, the clerk shrugging as he said with careless indifference,

"It's not ready yet, kid. The machine jammed—but almost."

"Almost" meant minutes to him, but to me, it was the difference between holding on to or losing an entire semester. I had delivered the file the day before, with clear instructions that it be *printed by 7:30 sharp. Everything had been calculated—timing, margins, test prints—and yet, I depended on someone who didn't seem to grasp what it meant. That sense—that my effort, my discipline, someone else's lateness could remove my entire obsession—filled me with a cold anger that still knots my stomach when I remember it.*

That day, I learned it wasn't enough to do things right. You had to make sure no one else held the last bit of control. It was a cruel lesson, one that followed me ever since like a shadow.

I nearly failed the class. I scraped by with a passing grade thanks to my previous work, but what stayed with me wasn't the grade—it was the sentence etched in my mind. I swore that never again—not even a delay that wasn't mine—would define me.

But I'm no longer in college. Now I'm responsible for projects that rise in real, inhabited spaces. I'm still in the unfinished lobby—thoughtful, tense—surrounded by dust and voices tangled with metal noise. And yet, the feeling is the same: that everything hangs by a thin thread, that any mistake—even one that isn't mine—could bring months of work crashing down.

My heart beats too fast. I try to breathe deeply, but the air cuts off before it reaches the bottom of my lungs. My shirt clings to my back with a cold sweat while my hands tremble—barely, but enough that I have to grip the blueprints harder than I should.

I try to calm myself by counting silently: one, two, three, four. But the numbers slip away, like fish I can't hold between my fingers. Anxiety gnaws at me from the inside; what scares me most isn't the mistake itself, but this feeling that I'm losing control.

I take a few steps away from the group of engineers, walking toward a corner where the shadows are denser and the noise is slightly muted. I lean against a bare concrete column and close my eyes. I can feel myself about to break.

I pull out my phone and type a short message, almost through clenched teeth:

"I'm about to break."

I don't think twice before sending it. The screen stays blank for a few endless seconds. I can feel my pulse in my temples—each beat pushing the wait forward like a dull knock. The noise of the site keeps going—hammers, voices, sparks of welding—but I'm suspended in that moment, alone with the echo of my thoughts floating in the air.

The phone vibrates. Allison replies:

"Matt, you're on the construction site, right? Don't move. I'm close. I'm coming over."

I slip the phone back into my pocket, but her words keep glowing in my mind as if they were still on the screen. I stay still, leaning against the concrete column, listening to the echo of the worksite—hammer blows, shouted orders, the metal squeal of a pulley. Everything feels distant, as if I were watching it all from the end of a tunnel.

I breathe, but the air doesn't reach all the way down. I run my hand along the rough edge of the column; dust clings to my fingers, leaving a gray smear. Counting doesn't help. Moving doesn't either. I just wait.

A few minutes later, I see her coming—helmet on, safety vest catching the light, walking with determination through the gravel and puddles of dry water. She doesn't ask anything; she doesn't need to. She walks straight to me and sets a hand on my arm.

"Let's go to the trailer, Matt. We can talk there."

The trailer smells of old coffee and damp air, like every construction office. Allison opens the door first and, with one brief look, clears the small meeting room where drawings and arguments usually fight for space. The two engineers inside get it immediately: they grab their things and leave without a word.

"Bring us two cold bottles of water, please," she tells the receptionist, who nods quickly and disappears.

I sit on one of the metal chairs, my back stiff, the blueprints still pressed against my chest like a shield. Allison sets her helmet on the table, rolls up her sleeves, and sits across from me. She doesn't speak yet. She just looks at me—with that mix of firmness and patience I find unbearable and necessary at once.

The receptionist returns a moment later, walking softly, as if her steps could disturb the air. She hands the bottles—first to Allison, then to me—and leaves the room, closing the door so softly it almost feels like it never closed at all, except that the noise of the site falls away all at once.

Allison twists the cap, takes a sip, and looks straight at me.

"Matt, if you keep pushing yourself this hard, something's going to snap. And I don't want to be here picking up the pieces."

I open my bottle clumsily; the plastic crackles too loudly in my hands. I take a long drink. The water is cold—it slides down my throat and settles in my stomach like a dead weight. I let her words echo while I wipe my mouth with the back of my hand.

"It's just..."—my voice shakes more than I want it to—"everything can fail, Allison. Everything. A delay, a late delivery, a calculation we didn't check enough. Do you know what it's like to have all the possible scenarios running through your head at once? It's like walking on glass: every step I take, I think it's about to crack."

She doesn't interrupt. She leans forward, elbows on the table, fingers interlaced, waiting. Her patience isn't passive—it's the most disarming kind of listening, the kind that forces me to spill everything out.

"I feel like there's never enough time, even when the reports say we're on schedule. I feel like the opening is tomorrow, and no one else sees it. That if I lose focus for a minute, everything will collapse... and it'll be my fault."

She finally speaks, her voice gentle, with a sharpness she doesn't bother to hide.

"What you're describing isn't the project, Matt. It's your head."

She leans forward and sets the iPad in the middle of the table, slowly, like she's laying down an essential card in a game neither of us can quit. She doesn't push it toward me or spin it around; she arranges it carefully, as though she knows even the way an object is moved can either calm or stir the air.

"Look at it with me," she says, almost in a whisper.

The screen casts a cool glow across the small meeting room. She scrolls through a page, then another. There's no hurry. Every movement of her finger across the glass seems designed to give me time to breathe.

"Slab pour: Friday," she murmurs, tracing the blue line that runs across the calendar.

A pause. She gives me space to take it in.

"Elevator installation: in progress." Another pause. "Mechanical systems: arriving Monday."

She lifts her gaze just enough to make sure I'm following. Her eyes don't demand anything; they simply stay with me.

"And the marble is already in production. The glass shipment is confirmed." She lets the silence fall for a moment, as if to be sure her words find a place inside my head.

I follow the colored lines on the screen. The calendar looks ordered, calm, like a musical score written with precision. My breathing is still uneven, but it no longer clashes with so much noise; there's a rhythm in those dates, a cadence she's quietly teaching me to see.

"Matt," she says at last, "we're not running behind time. We're carrying it with us."

She places her finger on a section further down the schedule and holds it there for a few seconds.

"See this?" she asks, still looking at the screen. "An entire week open before the inauguration. A full week just for contingencies."

The word "contingencies" tightens something inside me. She notices. She doesn't move her hand from the calendar; she keeps it there, steady.

"That's not a threat," she continues, her voice slow, almost wrapping around the air. "It's a gift. It means that if something goes wrong, we have room. You're not alone against the clock."

I feel the cold bottle between my hands. I squeeze it, rotate it, as if I needed something tangible to hold on to. I take another sip. The water helps me swallow the knot that still hasn't gone away.

She watches me without hurry. Takes a sip herself, sets the bottle down softly on the table, and rests her elbow on the back of her chair. She looks entirely in control of the moment, as if she knows that what I need most is for someone to breathe slower so I can remember how to do it.

"You don't have to carry everything on your back, Matt," she says at last, with a clarity that leaves no room for argument. "We're a team here."

Her words hang in the air for a moment—gentle but firm, like a hammer wrapped in velvet. And in the silence that follows, I feel my

163

chest open a little more. I breathe deeper this time. It's not complete relief, but it's the beginning of something.

Allison's words keep echoing: We're a team here. I nod, slowly,
as if I need to give each syllable room to settle in my head. I breathe
again. The air no longer stops halfway down my chest; it reaches a
little further, enough for my shoulders to ease.

She doesn't add anything right away. She gives me a few seconds that feel endless; seconds where the silence doesn't press
down but rests. The only sound is the air conditioner in the trailer,
the steady noise that used to irritate me and now turns into a neutral
hum.

"Look at me, Matt," she says finally.

I lift my head. Her eyes are steady, without hardness. They hold
mine without demanding.

"Everything you're feeling is real. I'm not going to take it away
with empty words. But I need you to see something: this building
doesn't depend on a thin thread. It depends on hundreds of hands
working with you. And those hands don't vanish just because you're
tired."

I close my eyes for a moment. I picture what she means: crews
pouring concrete, engineers studying blueprints, installers setting
ducts; everyone repeating their motions again and again with a precision that, until now, had only seemed limiting. But in her voice, it
becomes something else: a choreography that doesn't need my
constant supervision.

The cold bottle moistens my palms. I take another sip. This time
it isn't just to swallow a knot; it's to feel something cool down inside
me.

Allison picks up the iPad and sets it aside, as if closing a scene.

"We can go over the full schedule again if you want," she

says. "But the result will be the same: there's a margin. There's order. And there's trust."

She pauses.

"What there isn't," she adds, "is any reason for you to destroy yourself along the way."

Those words hit me softly, like a wave that doesn't knock you down but soaks you to the bone. I lean back in the chair. For the first time since we walked in, my hands let go of the blueprints. I set them on the table, open, as if they, too, needed to breathe.

She notices it and gives a slight nod, satisfied. There's no triumph in her expression—just calm. She takes one last sip of her water, caps the bottle, and rolls it slowly between her palms, marking some invisible rhythm.

"That's better," she whispers.

And I nod again—more easily this time, like someone who allows themselves to rest on a couch after a long day.

Allison stands up, takes her helmet from the table, and looks at me with a half-smile.

"Come on, Matt. Lunch is on me."

"Where to?" I ask, my voice still a little rough.

"There's a burger place nearby you're going to love," she says. "And you're in luck—it happens to be my favorite."

She winks, already heading for the door before I can come up with an excuse.

The restaurant smells of freshly baked bread and grilled meat—that deep, savory aroma that stirs your appetite without overwhelming you. The tables are light wood, polished to a soft sheen that reflects the warm glow of the hanging lamps. On the walls, black-and-white photographs of Texas landscapes and architectural details share space with framed neon signs, more decorative than loud. The floor, spotless, shines under the steady movement of waiters who move with almost choreographed precision.

The place breathes order and care, with an atmosphere that invites relaxation: a space designed so that something ordinary—a burger, a handful of fries—feels special. We sit in a corner by the window, where the life of the city filters in, though inside everything seems different: more leisurely, more friendly.

I understand why Alli likes this place. Everything sits exactly where it should, balanced between order and warmth—just like her.

A young waiter approaches with a notepad and a measured smile. Before I can speak, Allison takes the lead.

"Two Diet Cokes and two of the house specials, please."

I nod, a little surprised, and when the waiter walks away, I can't help raising an eyebrow at her.

"You ordered for me?"

She leans forward, that playful spark lighting her eyes.

"Matt." She gives me a mock-serious look, smiling just enough to warn me. "You're going to be impressed."

The waiter returns a few minutes later, carrying two trays that look heavier than they should. In front of me, he sets down a colossal burger: the brioche bun gleams as if freshly glazed, the thick patty drips juice along the edges, and a tiny skewer topped with a Texas flag holds the whole structure together. Two slices of cheddar melt over the sides, and the bacon glistens, making me want to dig in immediately. Beside it, a mountain of golden fries still sizzles faintly—so crisp they seem to crackle in the air before I even touch them. Too many, I think—almost a deliberate excess no one could finish.

We start eating in silence, as if each bite were conversation enough. The cheese stretches, the fries crunch, and for a moment, there's nothing in the world but flavor.

But Allison, even with her mouth half full, always finds room to surprise me.

So," she says, "when are you going to start dating again?"

The question catches me right in the middle of a bite. I cough, trying not to choke, and she bursts out laughing.

"What?" I manage, wiping my mouth with a napkin. "Where did that come from?"

"From my infinite wisdom," she says, shrugging. "And from the fact that you could use something in your life besides blueprints and checklists."

I snort, but she doesn't back off.

"Come on, tell me. What happened with the one who wanted to organize your life like a living agenda?"

I laugh, despite myself.

"Too much control. I already have my own schedules—I don't need an extra supervisor at home."

"Well said." She raises her hand for a high-five. "Next one...the free spirit."

"That one was... impossible." I make a small gesture of surrender. "Like chasing a paper airplane in a hurricane. I made plans, she changed them halfway through. There was no way to keep up."

"Sounds like she was having a lot more fun than you."

"Exactly." I give a crooked smile. "It wasn't a structural failure, just a design incompatibility."

Allison laughs so loudly that people at the following table turn to look.

"You're the only person who can turn love into structural analysis, Matt."

"Well, it's what I know."

She's still smiling, but this time she lowers her voice. She studies me for a moment longer than necessary, as if searching for a crack behind the joke.

"And Elena?"

The question catches me off guard. My breath stalls in my throat, as if the burger had stopped halfway down. I didn't expect it from her—not that directly, not with that name.

"You got me there," I say at last, setting the rest of the burger down on the plate. I sigh, look toward the window—anywhere but the weight of her stare. "She was everything I could've asked for in a woman... and I ruined it."

Allison doesn't look away. She doesn't soften the blow.

"Matt... sometimes it's not about ruining things," she says. "It's about learning."

The restaurant sounds stay the same—plates clinking, someone laughing at another table, the low music in the background—but her words cut through it all, clearer than anything else.

"You know," she adds, "I think you've changed. Before, I couldn't picture you holding a relationship together. Now I can."

"Why do you say that?"

"Because before, you only survived inside your head. Now, even if you still get lost there, at least you find your way back." She gestures toward me with open hands. "Like today."

I stay quiet, watching the condensation slide down my glass. She goes on, her tone softer now.

"I fight with those things too. My boyfriend and I... we're young, not thinking about marriage yet, but we still have our share of problems: silly jealousy, mismatched schedules, arguments over no-thing. It's not perfect. No relationship is."

She sighs, though her smile doesn't fade—it just curves with tenderness.

"Love isn't perfection, Matt. It's trying, over and over. It's waking up next to someone and being able to say, I'm still here."

Her words hang between us for a moment. I nod slowly, as if I need space for them to really sink in.

She takes one last bite of her burger, wipes her mouth with the napkin, then points it at me as if underlining her thought.

"And you deserve to try again, too. You're not the same man you were. Believe me."

The conversation drifts on so easily that I lose track of time. There's no rush. When we finish the burgers, we order coffee, and in that warm second round, everything feels even closer.

Allison spoke about her life with a kind of ease that she rarely shows.

She told me about her boyfriend, her plans, her fears—how sometimes she imagines a different future and then comes back to what she has because that's where she feels at peace.

She talked about her dreams, about how happy she is to be part of Divergent Holdings, about how much she's learned, and how proud she is of me.

I listened to her knowing that, in that moment, she wasn't the professional Allison who keeps the day running smoothly, but the personal one—the one who trusts, who allows herself just to be. What we have isn't just professional, or friendship, or admiration; it's the quiet certainty of wanting to see her grow without being hurt, as if somehow life itself had entrusted me with her care. Even if, most days, it feels like she's the one taking care of me.

And I understand now what she meant earlier. There was a time I wouldn't have been fully here—I would've hidden behind calculations, searching for excuses to escape. Not now. Now I can sit, share a meal, and laugh without rushing. I don't live only in my head anymore. I have friends. I can connect. I can learn from someone else. Even if I still falter, even if I still lose my way, at least now I know how to come back.

Allison drives me back to the site in her truck. The ride is short, just long enough for the silence between us to feel comfortable—as if the words had already done their job. The sun is setting, painting the city in a deep orange hue that slows everything down. When we arrive, the place is no longer the frenzy it was that morning. Only a few workers remain, storing their tools; the echo of a distant hammer fades in the air, and the cranes stand still, silhouetted against the lit sky.

We stop beside the trailer. Allison shifts into park and turns to me with a calm smile.

"See you tomorrow, Matt. Get some rest."

I nod. I don't say much, but I thank her—just enough to avoid that strange feeling of ingratitude. It's as if she's lent me a little of her calm to carry on. She gives me a brief pat on the shoulder. I step out, close the door gently, and watch her drive away, leaving me alone on the site.

I walk a few steps through the central courtyard. The noise is no longer an enemy; the silence of the empty site wraps around me like a long breath. The steel glows with copper light, and the shadows stretch until they become giants. Where I saw only chaos and deadlines a few hours ago, now I see promise. I picture the lobby completed—the light filtering softly, water falling slightly into the stone fountain. Everything is still standing, and so am I.

I head slowly toward my car. The gravel crunches under my sneakers, each step sounding different now that the site is quiet. The air smells of dust muted by dusk and of warm metal cooling down. I run my hand along the car's body, needing to feel that something familiar is waiting for me. I open the door; the soft creak breaks the stillness as I settle into the seat, my body grateful for the rest. I insert the key, turn it, and the engine roars to life with a deep rumble that contrasts with the calm surroundings. I take a deep breath, close the door, and shut the world out.

I pull out of the parking lot and head home. The traffic has eased; the city lights flicker on one by one, as if the night were lighting itself in layers. I drive in silence—no mental checklists, no pending tasks—just letting the wheel guide me while I breathe deeper than I thought possible.

The way home feels shorter than usual. The avenues pulse with a constant hum; streetlights and traffic signals cast shifting glows across the windshield, and for the first time in a long while, I don't mind driving without music. I just drive—the city unfolding like a curtain opening and closing as I pass. Calm doesn't arrive all at once—it comes in waves: with every green light, every familiar corner, every breath that no longer stumbles.

When I open the door, Toby runs toward me with an enthusiasm that doesn't understand schedules or deadlines. His paws thump against the floor, his tail cutting the air like a happy metronome. I kneel and hold him close, burying my face in his warm fur. The world narrows to that simple moment—no one asking, no one expecting. Toby, with his boundless loyalty, reminds me there are things I don't need to calculate.

"Thank you, buddy," I whisper, looking directly into his tender eyes. "You have no idea how much you hold me together, Toby. No matter how the world keeps turning, you're always here, faithful, whole. I love you, and I'm so grateful you are part of my life."

I hold him a moment longer and smile, quietly confident that, little by little, I'm beginning to feel like I belong to this world.

10 Foundations of Life

The road to Frisco no longer feels as long as it did the first time. The highway, flat and straight, carries me without hurry, as if it knows I am not here to supervise anything today, only to observe.

It is one of my favorite moments—coming at this stage, when everything is still bare bones, and yet my mind insists on dressing it. Where there are twisted rods, I already imagine hallways cut by diagonal light; where there is only removed soil, I see tables, voices, footsteps crossing. It is a strange privilege to watch a project under construction and, at the same time, see it inhabited in my imagination. As if the present and the future were walking side by side, separated only by a thin layer of dust.

Allison and Samuel were here yesterday, finalizing installation details, tending to whatever always seems urgent. I came alone. I needed to see with my own eyes how the project is beginning to take shape as the place that will become VitaPlaza.

I park beside the construction trailers—those white rectangles that always seem temporary but feel like part of the landscape here. I turn off the engine and stay inside for a moment, watching the movement on the other side of the windshield: yellow helmets coming and going, dust rising with every step, a crane swinging slowly, in rhythm with the whole scene.

I open the door and the heat rushes in, wrapping around me, but it no longer intimidates me as it once did. I walk slowly, the invisible blueprints still pulsing in my memory, and I hear the voices calling out to me: "Morning, Architect!" "Glad to have you here." They greet me with a natural ease that surprises me every time, as if my presence were more than supervision—a reminder that this project beats in many hearts, not only in mine.

As I approach, the machines keep roaring, diesel engines trembling in the hot air, but the scene is no longer the dusty chaos of that first visit. Where once there was only dust and promise, columns now rise, walls trace the outlines of corridors, and a central courtyard is taking shape.

Among the dust, palm trees and newly planted trees peek out, massive and transplanted, with roots wrapped in damp burlap. Still held upright by their braces, they already cast their first shadows over the gravel. I recognize something of myself in them. Moved, tied down, forced to take root in new ground. At first, they seem fragile, out of place, but I know that one day they will stand firm, and no one will remember they were not born here. Perhaps belonging is just that—enduring the first wind until the shadow feels like home.

I walk a little further and let my gaze dissolve into the weave of steel and dust. Before, every step was a reminder of risk, of how fragile an idea can be. Today, though, every detail speaks of endurance. The tensile canopies still hold, and with them, VitaPlaza's heart beats stronger. It was never a whim; it was a pulse we fought to protect. This time, I don't feel the vertigo of losing everything, but the calm of having held the vision together with a team that refused to let it break. This place will become what we dreamed—a heart of shade and life in the middle of the desert.

A young engineer approaches as soon as he sees that I stop in front of the central courtyard. His shirt is soaked with sweat and his tablet is covered with dust, yet there's no trace of exhaustion on his face—only a brightness I recognize.

"Architect," he calls out, raising his voice above the noise of the mixer, "I was just looking for you. We've been checking the membrane junctions, and there's a detail that's bothering me."

He points to the tablet screen: a schematic rendering filled with red notes. He explains that the supplier wants to shift one of the anchor points slightly to save on steel.

"See here?" he says, zooming in on the plan with his fingers. "It could still work, but I'm afraid we might lose tension in this corner."

I listen in silence. My eyes drift from the screen to the real structure, still incomplete, where the cables stretch out like metallic veins. I imagine the wind moving through them, the shadow spreading like a wing across the courtyard. I take a slow breath before answering.

"If we move that anchor," I say at last, "the shadow will lose its continuity. It isn't a whim. The line needs to stay clean—unbroken."

The engineer nods quickly, as if he'd been waiting for that response to confirm what he already knew.

"I thought so, Architect, but I needed to hear it from you."

He pauses, then smiles. "This project feels different. I've worked on plazas all my life, and they always seem the same. Not on this one. Here, you can tell something is truly being cared for."

I pause for a moment, processing his words, surprised by their honesty. I usually brush off comments like that, but today I find myself accepting them with quiet calm.

"We don't do this alone," I reply, pointing to the blueprint on his tablet. "You, me... everyone. Every decision adds up to help this place breathe."

He nods again, more firmly this time. He jots down a quick note on the screen before stepping back with a respectful gesture.

"Thank you, Architect. Now I can move on."

I watch him walk away through the rebar and piles of gravel. I think that, in a way, this is the real work—not just the walls rising around us, but the convictions that keep us standing.

I keep walking toward the wing where the stores will rise. There are no finished walls yet, only steel frames and blocks outlining uneven corridors, with heaps of gravel interrupting the path. Yet, the intention is already visible. It isn't an endless row of identical boxes, like those outlets that trade experience for multiplication. Here, each space will have its own height, its own pause, its own proportion. Some more expansive, some taller, some with windows ready to catch the afternoon light. I want each to have its own voice and, together, form a conversation, not a monotone chorus.

As I walk among the bare frames, I feel how the air circulates differently in each section. Some corridors feel enclosed, intimate; others open with the promise of spaciousness. It's as if I can already hear the echo of footsteps, the sound of displays being arranged, the murmur of conversations that do not yet exist.

I continue my round, and in one of the corridors ahead, a supervisor stops me. An older man, with a neatly trimmed gray mustache, a weathered face, crisp white shirt tucked in with care, and a white helmet, like everyone else on the construction site. His boots, clean despite the dust, shine as if freshly polished. He only needs a cowboy hat to look the part. He carries a tablet in his hand but holds it like an old clipboard. His pace is unhurried, measured.

"Architect," he says, tipping his head slightly, "I was waiting for you so I could show you something."

He points to the line of stores half-built, some with higher roofs, others with narrower fronts.

"With the changes in height and volume," he explains, "the wiring could become a problem. You had already asked that nothing be left exposed, but with these differences, we risk ending up with messy junctions and visible cable trays in certain sections."

He shows me the conflict points on the tablet. The image is clear. Those details could blemish the purity of the design.

"We could propose a technical corridor along the back," he adds. "A uniform, concealed strip that lets us run all the infrastructure while keeping the clean design. That way, each store keeps its character, but the power and data stay tidy, orderly, and out of sight."

I study him for a moment and nod.

"I hadn't seen it that way on the blueprints," I admit. "Thank you for pointing it out. A slip like this could cost us the harmony of the whole."

I take out my phone, photograph the rendering and the structure in front of us, and send them to Samuel with a quick note:

"Check the rear technical corridor. Update the design before we go any further."

The supervisor smiles slightly, satisfied that his observation hasn't gone unnoticed.

"Thank you," I say, slipping the phone back into my pocket. "Sometimes we cling so tightly to the overall vision that the small fissures slip past us."

And I appreciate that you listen," he replies in a calm voice. "Not everyone does. It's easy to hold on to a sheet of paper and forget what the construction site itself is trying to say."

We shake hands. His grip is firm and dry—the handshake of someone who's been doing this for years. As he walks away, I think about how in those invisible details—the cables no one sees, the conduits that never appear in photographs—lies the real difference between a space that feels chaotic and one that breathes.

I walk toward the central courtyard, the one I had imagined as the heart of the project since the first blueprints. No canopies are billowing yet, but the first steel posts are already in place. They rise at measured angles, like spears waiting for fabric to turn them into wings. At their base, the reflecting pools begin to take shape—not rigid rectangles or predictable circles, but broken, irregular forms that seem to stretch farther than they genuinely do, as if the water itself wished to deceive the eye and offer a more generous horizon.

I stop a moment in front of them. I remember the discussions, the nights spent over blueprints, the simulations that seemed to push against us. And yet here they are, firm, anchored—not all on costly independent foundations, but some integrated into the very structure of the building.

It was Samuel who proposed it quietly that afternoon:

"If we anchor to the existing roofs and frames, we'll save both work and money, and reinforce the sense of continuity."

At first, I hesitated, afraid the aesthetics might suffer, but now I see the posts as if they had always belonged here. What once seemed a compromise now reveals itself as a triumph: the structure speaks a single language, free of forced seams.

The savings were no small thing—I know that. Weeks of work, tons of steel, budgets pulled tight like ropes. But more than the numbers, what I feel is pride. This idea survived not only through stubbornness but also through shared ingenuity. It wasn't imposition; it was dialogue.

I lift my eyes and try to picture the fabric stretched between the posts, taut against the wind, casting its shade across the courtyard. I can almost hear the water murmuring as it slides through the newly designed mirrors, see the reflections multiplying the space, and feel the cool air that does not yet exist. This is more than architecture; it is a refuge from haste and sun, a reminder that even in the heart of the desert, there can be reprieve.

The site demands no explanations, asks no unanswerable questions. It only invites me to stand still and watch as the impossible begins to take shape. The old vertigo fades, replaced by something rare in me: confidence.

I find myself silent, alone with the crunch of my boots on gravel and the distant hum of the work around me. And in that stillness, I understand that this space, though still bare, already beats as I imagined it would—a heart of shadow and water, ready to offer a sense of belonging.

My pocket vibrates.

The phone's sharp sound shatters the moment like a stone thrown at a mirror.

I pull it from my pocket. The name on the screen catches me off guard: Dave.

Dave and everyone who knows me understands I'm not fond of calls. I prefer messages: brief, stripped of extras. That's why his name flashing there unsettles me. If he's calling, it must be important.

For a second, I think about letting it ring out, but something in me knows I should answer.

"Dave?" I say, trying to sound casual.

But his voice isn't like it usually is. It's deeper, heavier, carrying a weight I've never heard before.

"Do you have time today, Matt? I need to talk to you."

Dave greets me at the door with a tired but genuine smile. His handshake is firm before he steps aside to let me in.

"Come on in, Matt."

I cross the threshold and pause, caught off guard.

The room is spacious, and every detail seems designed to steady whoever walks through the door. The desk sits at the far end—old, solid wood, marked by time. Its edges have softened with age, its grain revealing an oak no furniture catalog could ever reproduce.

Bookshelves line two full walls—old but immaculate—lit by small lamps that cast indirect light. Between volumes of philosophy, psychology, fiction, history, and architecture, there are gaps filled with curious objects: a rusted compass, a nameless clay figurine, a framed paper airplane, a few toys, a clock forever stopped at 3:20. Each seems to hold a story never told. Most, I suspect, are gifts from patients—tokens that need no explanation to express gratitude.

The sitting area fills a bright corner of the office. Two brown leather armchairs rest on a red Persian rug, the kind where every arabesque feels like an unfinished tale. Light filters through wooden blinds, letting the late afternoon in as golden lines that trace patterns across the rug's weave. I take in the angles, the proportions of the furniture, the measured height of the ceiling: everything speaks of welcome without pretension. It isn't a solemn or imposing place, but an intimate refuge—designed, whether intentionally or not, to make anyone feel comfortable the moment they sit down to talk.

"Dave, I don't know why I've never been to your office before... You have a unique space."

I say it almost without thinking, because it's true. The air feels fresh, pleasant, as if the walls themselves had learned to care for those who enter.

Dave gives a small smile and leads me to his desk. He settles into his large black leather chair, which creaks softly beneath him, and gestures for me to take one of the two matching chairs across from him.

He leans back slightly, fingers interlaced over his lap, and looks at me with that mix of curiosity and warmth that always disarms me.

"So," he says, slowly, without hurry, "how's VitaPlaza going?"

He says it as if inviting me to unfold the memory with care. It isn't the question of a casual acquaintance—it's the question of a friend who wants to hear how something inside me still beats.

I smile at the thought of the morning.

"I was there today," I tell him. "Walked through the whole site, saw the first trees casting shade... and I caught myself feeling calm. I worked directly on it—went over a few questions, made some adjustments—but it was different this time. No anxiety, no rushing. I just enjoyed watching it slowly stop being a construction site and start becoming a place. I liked it, Dave. I could imagine it alive."

He nods slowly, like someone receiving good news from a dear friend. He stays quiet a moment longer than usual, and then his voice drops deeper.

"And... the big project?"

He doesn't say it as if referring to "another" project, but as if naming something sacred—a heart beating on its own.

I take a deep breath.

"That one... It's just around the corner. Time's pressing, the days are numbered. But we're doing well—everything's in order."

I pause, look at him directly, wearing that mix of fatigue and pride that only he understands.

"Want to know what I'm going to call it?"

Dave raises his eyebrows slightly, as if the question had opened an unseen door.

"Of course I do."

"Divergent One," I say finally, almost in a whisper, as if the name needed to come out slowly, to adjust to the air before it could belong to the world.

He smiles—not in surprise, but with the calm of someone who knows a word like that will stick.

"Yes... that name has roots. That name will stay. Divergent One. I love it."

I stay quiet for a moment after hearing the name in Dave's voice, as if the echo hung in the air between us. Then I smile, a little shy.

"Dave... you know how much you mean to me. Your place, and your family's, is already set to be as close to me as possible that day."

I say it with an open heart, my tone naïve, almost childlike, waiting for his response.

"You'll be there, right?"

Dave rests his hands on the arms of his chair and nods at once, as if he didn't need to think about it.

"Of course, Matt. I wouldn't miss it for anything. You have no idea how much I want to be there, to see you standing in front of everyone, presenting what you've always dreamed of."

His words bring me peace, as they always do. We talk for a few more minutes, without rush; we review dates, details, and the inevitability of exhaustion. Everything seems normal, and yet there's a different pause, a faint shadow in the way he looks toward the window before answering, as if part of him were somewhere else.

Then I remember why I'm really here—the unexpected call just hours ago. The conversation starts to fill with silences, and in those silences, I realize I didn't come just to talk about projects.

I stay quiet for a moment, then speak plainly.

"Dave, I'm glad we're talking about all this—you know how much it means to me—but today I don't feel this is about me. I'm worried about you. It's not like you to call, though I'm glad you did... tell me, what's going on?"

Dave takes a moment before answering. He turns his chair toward the window, as if searching for words among the golden lines the sun casts through the blinds. When he finally speaks, his voice is not that of the confident psychologist nor that of the friend who always has advice ready. It's another voice—lower, rougher.

"Matt... I'm fifty-five years old."

He stops, as if testing the weight of that number in the air.

"And my kids... they're still so little."

He falls silent—letting the chair creaks, a faint complaint that sounds almost like a sigh.

"It scares me," he goes on. "It scares me not to have the energy to keep up with them. That one day, they'll run faster than I can follow. Or that time won't be enough for me to see them succeed."

He pauses again. The clock on the shelf—the one stopped at 3:20—seems to stare at us, reminding us that time always slips away.

"I wake up in the middle of the night and think: Will I make it to Emma's graduation? Will I be there when Lucas decides who he wants to be? And I don't know, Matt. I just don't know."

His voice breaks for a moment, but he doesn't turn his head. He doesn't try to hide it.

I stay still, holding the silence with him. I understand it isn't my turn to speak, but to listen.

Dave brings a hand to his chin, as if trying to hold onto the words before letting them go.

"Matt, let me tell you a story that's marked me all my life..."

He leans back slightly in the chair, and for a moment, it feels as though I'm no longer sitting across from a fifty-five-year-old man, but from a boy who still doesn't quite understand what absence means.

"My father died when I was barely two years old. I never really got to know him. What I have are the stories others gave me—that he had a smile that lit up a room, that his boots were always left at the entrance, that he said my name with immense pride. But I don't remember him. There are no scenes of us together. I grew up on borrowed memories, like a puzzle with missing pieces.

As a child, I felt more like a shadow than a memory. At school, when I saw other kids with their fathers at events, I used to search for mine among the crowd, even though I already knew he wouldn't be there. I stayed beside my mother—always steady, always radiant—carrying the weight alone.

My mother was the best thing life could have given me. She worked twice, three times as hard to keep us going. She would rise before dawn and come home long after dark, exhausted, yet still had a smile for me. She taught me to be brave, to get up, to not complain. She was mother and father in one body, and even then... she could never invent the figure I was missing. She could never have that deep voice that said, 'I'm here, son.'

That emptiness stayed with me. I learned to live with it, learned to disguise it, but it never stopped hurting. Even though I grew up surrounded by love, the absence was always there. And now, as a father myself, that same emptiness is what scares me most—that one day, Emma and Lucas will have to live with the shadow instead of my presence."

I watched him closely. I saw how his eyes, usually steady and attentive, began to turn glassy, as if releasing reflections that he had kept hidden for too long. His voice faltered, dragging each word as though it weighed more than he could bear. Even his body—the same one I had always seen upright and self-assured—seemed to sink a little into the chair, as if memory itself were pressing him down.

Before me was no longer the psychologist who understands everything, nor the strong friend who always finds a way out. There sat a man stripped bare by his own story. I realized I could be a friend to him now—a confidant, someone he could lean on—just as he had so often been for me.

Silence stretched between us, heavy yet calm, like a mantle neither of us tried to lift. There was no need for words; his vulnerability had already said enough. And in that pause, something struck me: even someone as strong and wise as Dave—the man who had held me up so many times—also carries cracks and fears. I am not the only one with shadows. And now I know I never was.

We stayed quiet for a while, until I chose to break the silence— not to disturb the moment, but to join him in it. I leaned forward slightly, searching for his eyes.

"Dave... can I tell you something?" I asked softly.

He blinked, as if returning from a distant thought, and managed a faint, tired, but genuine smile.

"Of course, Matt. You always can."

"For you, what has it meant to be a father? To have a family, to share your life with them... what has it truly given you?"

Dave froze for a moment, surprised by the direction of the question. Then he sighed, rested his hands on the armchairs, and his expression softened.

"Everything, Matt. Absolutely everything. That's what I'm afraid of losing…"

"Dave," I began quietly, "I understand your fear. I understand that feeling that time is slipping away. But let me tell you something: what you already give your children is precious, more than precious. You're there. And what stays with them isn't the number of days, but the mark you leave in every day you share with them."

He looks up slightly, as if he hadn't expected those words.

"It isn't the counted hours that shape Emma and Lucas," I go on, "but what they see in you—your presence, your example, your way of loving them. That… that's what stays."

A long silence. Dave nods slowly, as though testing the truth in every word. He runs a hand across his forehead and exhales, as if releasing an old weight.

"Sometimes you forget, Dave," I add, "that not everything is measured in years or energy. It's measured in presence. I've seen how Emma runs to you, how Lucas watches you when you speak… those things don't come from time or strength—they're born from love. And that, you've already planted in them."

He looks down and smiles slightly, as if trying to convince himself it's true.

"I don't know if I see it that way, Matt." He sighs. "I always think about what's missing—what could go wrong."

"And I'm always thinking about what I'm missing," I say with a brief ironic gesture. "But I admire you, Dave. I mean that. I admire the way you are with your family—the way you're a light for your kids. I don't have that, I don't have a family of my own, but seeing you reminds me it's still possible to leave a mark on the people we love."

His eyes fill with tears. He doesn't look away. He meets my gaze, and I know he's listening.

"Matt," he says finally, his voice calmer now, "thank you. You don't know what it means to hear that from you. I know you've always seen me as the strong one, but today was one of those days when you feel you're the weakest. Sometimes all I need is this—to be reminded that what I do will outlast me."

The silence that follows isn't heavy—it's warm. And then, as if something rekindled inside him, he meets my eyes with renewed steadiness.

"But now it's my turn."

"How's it my turn, Dave?" I interrupt, leaning forward with a hint of a smile. "You're always there for me. You're the one who gives advice, who listens, who holds me up. You have to let others listen to you, too, so they can help you. You've become a real friend and a guide to me, and now I see it goes both ways."

He smiles slightly, as if those words had landed exactly where he needed them.

"Dave, you're still young. Maybe not as young as I am," I say with a teasing laugh that loosens the air between us, "but you've still got so much life ahead. You take care of yourself, you eat well, and you've got all the love of your family. I'm sure you'll live many more years and get to enjoy every stage with your kids. You'll probably show up at Emma's graduation with a cane—but I know you'll be there, watching her succeed with the same pride you speak of her now."

I fall silent for a moment.

"Life's a mystery, we both know it. We're here today, maybe

gone tomorrow. But what I've learned most from you is to live each day as if it were the last, to enjoy the present without getting trapped in what's missing."

Dave lowers his head for a moment, as if turning my words over, then lets out a short laugh—not mocking, but relieved.

"A cane, huh?" he says, shaking his head. "Maybe so... but if I show up with a cane, I'll make sure it's with a new suit too."

We both laugh, and the tension breaks just enough for the air to feel lighter. Dave takes advantage of the pause to lean back in his chair. His gaze is once again the one that's held me so many times—steady, clear, with tenderness hidden behind every word.

"But now," he says, "it is my turn."

He pauses, letting the silence settle.

"Matt, I've seen how you've changed. Before, you'd drift off—you'd disappear into your own head, and it was hard to bring you back. But now... now you find your way back. And believe me, that alone makes all the difference."

His words strike me gently, like a truth I needed to hear.

"You don't have to change who you are, Matt," he continues. "That stubborn mind of yours—with all its layers, its angles, its silences—that's what makes you create the way you do. That's what makes you unique. It's not about suppressing that or forcing yourself to fit where you don't belong. It's about learning how to stay connected to the world without losing yourself in the process."

He pauses for a moment. His voice softens, as if he were placing the final piece of a mosaic with care.

"You've come a long way—further than you sometimes allow yourself to believe. But I want to ask you for something: take one more step. Find someone to walk with you in this—a psychologist, a therapist who isn't me. I'm your friend, and I always will be. But I know you can go even further if you let yourself be accompanied professionally, too."

Dave rests his hands on the desk and looks straight at me.

"Do it, Matt. Not because you can't do it alone, but because you don't have to."

I rub my face, take a deep breath, and meet his gaze with a crooked smile.

"Well, yeah, Dave, I get it... But tell me something—don't you think that, with you, I'm killing two birds with one stone? You're my therapist and my friend... full service!"

He lets out a genuine laugh, the kind that fills the room. Shaking his head, amused, he then leans toward me with that clarity he never loses.

No, Matt. That's exactly the point. As your friend, I can walk beside you, laugh with you, and even tell you the uncomfortable truths. But I can also miss things—angles that another therapist, someone who's only your psychologist, would see with more objectivity."

He pauses, his tone softer now.

"Friendship can be a filter, and that's precisely what makes it so valuable. But there are things an outside voice can help you see—without the layer of affection I'll always have for you."

I stay quiet, letting his words find their place in me. Dave stays silent too, but this time it isn't a heavy silence. It's one of those that feel right, as if it belonged to the conversation itself. The air in the office seems different, lighter, as though simply sharing our vulnerability had opened an invisible window.

He exhales, leans back in his chair, and smiles with a weary grin.

"Well, Matt, that's enough depth for one day. You're about to make me cry more than my patients do... It almost feels like you're the one who should be sitting in my chair today."

The laughter that follows is pure, unexpected. It breaks through the lingering tension like glass shattering—only without harm. We both laugh, softly at first, then louder, until the office fills with it, losing for a moment its usual seriousness.

Dave settles back in his seat, runs a hand across the desk as if organizing his thoughts, and gives me a knowing look.

"Do you remember the first time we met? That empty restaurant, the one that felt like they were about to close it just for us..."

He pauses dramatically, raising his eyebrows.

"How packed it was that day! There were... hmm... how many of us? Two?"

His joke lingers in the air for a second, and I can't help but burst out laughing. I lean forward, resting one arm on the desk, shaking my head.

"Yes, Dave. And if I remember right, I ordered the same thing I always order from James... and you, not wanting to make things awkward, said with the utmost seriousness, 'The same as him. And the wine? The same as him too.' You said it so seriously, straightening the silverware like it was a ritual."

He laughs too, and for a moment we're both back at that table—as if time had folded in on itself and we could see our younger selves again, unaware of the friendship taking root right then.

The laughter fades slowly, not abruptly, but like a fire settling into embers. Dave nods, the smile still hanging on his lips.

"And we've stayed in that same spot at the bar ever since, Matt. Sometimes with different plates, but always the same conversation."

His words stop me. There's no solemnity in his tone, yet there's a quiet truth that cuts deep. I look at him and know he's right. I no longer see him only as the brilliant psychologist or the mentor who always finds a way. I see him for what he really is: a friend—with his cracks and his strength, his fears and his wisdom.

The clock on the shelf seems to look at us again, not now as a reminder of time slipping away, but as a witness to what is happening here—in the rhythm of words and laughter.

In my mind, the metaphor draws itself: every conversation with him is like laying another brick in an invisible building—one that appears in no blueprint or model, yet holds as firmly as any column.

That building is called life, held together by friendships like ours, that hold more than they reveal.

Humberto M. Sotomayor

11 Divergent One

The house still holds the silence of dawn. It's not quite night, yet the day hasn't fully arrived. Light filters shyly through the blinds, drawing thin lines across the wooden floor. Outside, the city is beginning to stir: a garbage truck rumbling at the corner, the hum of a car rushing past, a distant dog barking at the wind. Inside, though, everything feels suspended, as if the walls themselves knew that today is different.

In the living room, the air still carries the faint aroma of the coffee I made, untouched and still waiting. I left it in the kitchen, forgotten in its cup, cooling slowly as if it had all the time in the world. The coffee table is neat—too neat—with papers aligned, the sofa clear, the lamp lit since before dawn.

I head upstairs and find Toby asleep in his little bed, surrounded by stuffed animals and toys. His steady breathing keeps a rhythm different from the clock's—a rhythm that knows nothing of grand openings or press events, only of calm.

I step into the dressing room and stop in front of the mirror. The reflection stares back with a face I don't quite recognize: a crisp white shirt, a dark gray suit still carrying the scent of the dry cleaner, a black tie perfectly knotted. I run my hand along the collar, feeling the tight fabric. That top button always feels like it's choking me, suffocating me, binding me. I think about how far this ritual is from my actual uniform: dusty work boots, a white helmet, and an iPad stained with coffee. My domain has always been among gravel, not red carpets.

I straighten the suit jacket once more—the fabric shimmering under the bathroom light. "It's a disguise," I think, but a necessary one. Today I can't show up with graphite-stained hands. Today, I'm not just representing myself, but an entire team, a vision raised layer by layer. And though it makes me uncomfortable, the thought of not being impeccable feels worse.

Toby wakes and barks behind me, as if to wish me good morning. When he was a puppy, the faintest sound of me heading to the kitchen would wake him, and he'd follow close behind. Now, as an old dog, he prefers to rest until his body tells him otherwise. He trails after me from room to room, as if he's on a mission to supervise every move. He sits in the doorway, tilts his head, and looks at me with those eyes that seem to ask whether I really need to dress like this. As I pass, I pet him, and in his calm, I find a serenity no suit can provide.

I stop again in the living room. I adjust my jacket, check my watch, and straighten a folder that didn't need it. It's a useless ritual, but it calms my nerves.

Each small gesture gives me the illusion of control on a day that will be full of cameras, voices, and applause that I still don't know how to receive.

The phone vibrates on the table. The screen lights up with a message—Allison:

> "It's time to head out. Today's a big day for the whole team. I'll be waiting."

I smile without meaning to. She always knows exactly what to say— nothing extra, no embellishment. It's her way of reminding me that this isn't just mine, that we are a true "we", and that no inauguration means anything unless it's lived in the plural.

I bend down toward Toby, scratch behind his ears, and he answers with a slow wag of his tail, as if he understands more than he lets on.

"Wish me luck, little buddy," I whisper. "You know I need it."

I step outside. The cool morning air hits my face, so different from the regulated air of the living room. At the window, Toby watches me for a moment before curling back into place. It's a silent ritual—a farewell repeated every time I cross the door.

The day is just beginning, and I know it will be long—filled with emotion and, I hope, with joy.

I get into the car and close the door shut, the sound echoing more than I expected. For an instant, I stay still, hands on the wheel, watching my reflection in the windshield: gray suit, tightened tie—a version of myself I'm still learning to recognize.

I turn the key. The engine stirs with a low, steady hum, as if it knows there's no turning back.

The usual drive to the office feels different today. The streets seem longer, the traffic lights slower. Every stop is a reminder of what awaits me: a crowded lobby, voices, cameras, handshakes. I've never liked crowds, never felt comfortable being watched, and yet today it can't be avoided.

I catch myself sweating in my palms, despite the air conditioning. I take a deep breath, trying to match my rhythm to the white line repeating ahead of me. Each mark becomes a count: one, two, three, four... as if the road itself could calm me.

The city drifts by unhurriedly—familiar buildings, parks where I once stopped to walk, streets breathing their own rhythm among early cyclists and cars that seem to float in a distant cadence. On one corner, a bakery just opened releases the aroma of warm dough; farther on, sunlight flashes against windshields in brief sparks. And amid that parade of everyday scenes comes a quiet certainty: it all began with a drawing. A house sketched in crayons on paper, with crooked shadows and impossible windows. That childish outline was the beginning of a path that now leads me here, to inaugurate an entire vision.

I feel a stir in my stomach. Nerves, yes—but also something else: the awareness that what I once dreamed with a child's hands now breathes on its own.

The car descends the ramp into the underground parking. The white ceiling lights flick on in sequence, one after another, as if marking my arrival. The concrete smells new—a rough mix of fresh paint, dry dust, and newly placed metal. I turn off the engine. The silence that follows is unlike any I've known on a worksite. No hammers, no drills—just a clean echo, almost solemn, as if the building itself were waiting in stillness.

I walk toward the elevator. The polished floor reflects my steps, and for a moment, I feel like a visitor, not the architect. The button glows a soft amber under my finger; the doors open without a sound, just a discreet, elegant slide. The elevator ascends slowly, as if giving me time to take in what's about to come.

When the doors open, the lobby greets me all at once. Water already runs along the stone wall—a steady thread filling the air with a fresh murmur. The skylight filters the light in perfect diagonals that fall across the marble, and each shadow seems to move with a life of its own. The air conditioning isn't a forced gust but an invisible breeze that follows the rhythm of the water.

I'm taken aback and delighted at the same time. It feels like I dreamed it—not as blueprints or renderings, but as a living refuge. It's still empty. Only a few staff members are there, quietly adjusting cables, testing microphones, and aligning chairs. The space, though ready for a crowd, pulses serenely. It feels like a theater just minutes before the curtain rises. And for a moment, I am its only spectator.

The murmur of the water surrounds me when another sound breaks through—quick footsteps, heels tapping lightly across the floor. I look up, and there's Allison. Her smile shines brighter than the skylight itself. She's walking fast, as if she can't contain her excitement, and as soon as she sees me, she raises her hand and quickens her pace.

"Matt!" she exclaims, and before I can react, she wraps me in a firm hug—one that feels more like a celebration than a greeting.

Her voice trembles with joy.

"It's incredible… seeing it like this, in person. You dreamed it, drew it a thousand times, and now—it's here!"

I stay silent for a moment. I watch her glow with that effortless energy of hers, and I realize she's right—today, the impossible became real.

When she steps back, I notice she isn't alone. Beside her stands a man about her age, calm in demeanor, his gentle expression a contrast to Allison's unstoppable presence. She takes his hand naturally and draws him closer.

"I want you to meet someone. This is Daniel," she says, her eyes sparkling with pride. "My boyfriend."

I extend my hand, surprised. I'd heard his name in passing—a brief mention during a meeting or that day we talked over burgers—but I'd never met him. He shakes my hand firmly and nods with quiet respect.

"I've heard a lot about you, Matt."

His voice is calm, serene—the kind of tone that understands he's stepping into a space that matters to her.

"I hope it wasn't all bad," I reply with a small smile, enough to draw a short laugh from both of them.

Allison steps forward, gesturing broadly toward the lobby.

"It looks even more impressive as it fills up, doesn't it?" she says, and her eyes carry the same pride I feel, but with a freedom I've never learned to express.

Samuel arrives with his usual composure: shirt perfectly pressed, folder under his arm, that steady, technical calm that never falters, not even at opening events. He doesn't smile much, but his eyes give him away—there's a gleam, a restrained pride.

"Architect," he greets, with a slight nod, as always, though his tone today carries a rare warmth.

I shake his hand firmly and let out a brief laugh.

"'Architect'? You know I'm Matt. Save the title for the press, not for me."

Samuel raises an eyebrow, serious only in appearance.

"I say it out of respect, not protocol. But fine... Matt."

The pause he makes before saying my name sounds almost like a joke.

"I couldn't miss seeing this come to life for the first time," he adds, and for a moment his composed expression softens. He looks up toward the light falling from the skylight and says quietly, "It's alive, Matt. Just as you imagined it."

He doesn't say more—he's never been one for speeches—but those words, "it's alive", carry more weight than any magazine feature ever could.

The hum of the lobby grows: people arriving, greetings, a photographer trying to stay unnoticed as he adjusts his lens. And then I see them—Dave and Sarah walking together, with Emma and Lucas a few steps ahead. The children enter as if the place already belonged to them, amazed by the water spilling down the stone wall and the shadows tracing patterns on the floor. Emma tilts her face toward the light and smiles; Lucas runs toward the reflecting pool, mesmerized by the movement of his own reflection.

"Dad, look!" he shouts, his voice blending with the murmur of the water until it becomes part of the space itself.

Dave walks more slowly, with that calm dignity that always seems to follow him. His eyes take in every corner, as if he wants to be sure he misses nothing. When he reaches me, he extends his hand firmly.

"Matt," he says, his voice deep but filled with emotion, "I have no words. This... this is extraordinary."

Sarah smiles beside me, warm and genuine as always. Emma comes over and gives me a quick, spontaneous hug, while Lucas keeps chasing the shadows across the floor.

In that moment—with them here, with Allison, Samuel, and Dave around me—I feel something I rarely allow myself to feel: the building is no longer mine. It now belongs to them too, to those who carried it with me every step of the way.

The lobby begins to fill with faces beyond the familiar ones. Dark suits, elegant dresses, cameras hanging quietly from the necks of journalists who greet one another, shaking hands as they search for the best angle. You can feel the air shifting—from the soft murmur of a few voices to a steady hum, like a river that won't stop growing. Light glances off the marble, the water along the wall keeping time with its unchanging rhythm.

I approach a few guests with a brief smile and measured words: "Welcome." "Thank you for coming." Then I step back, letting the team—Allison radiant, Samuel flawless—take over the more extended conversations. I observe. And what I see is enough: people walking without hurry, lifting their eyes toward the skylight, pausing in front of the water as if they'd found a moment of calm in the middle of the day.

A photographer crouches down to capture Lucas playing with his reflection. Emma reaches up to touch the beam of light coming from above, as if she could hold it. The adults talk in small clusters, but the children seem to be the first to understand the meaning of this place: that here, everything breathes.

I stand off to the side, almost invisible among the crowd. I don't mind being on the margins. The building has begun to breathe on its own. It no longer needs me to present it—it's presenting itself.

A group of young people waits in the lobby, perfectly aligned, as if they had rehearsed punctuality itself. Light gray suits, blue ties, matching the badges that read "HOST" in discreet lettering. Each holds a tablet, carrying the composed posture of someone who understands that today is not just about showing a building—it's about presenting an idea made real.

The guests begin to gather around them. I watch as one of the hosts points toward the skylight, another explains the arrangement of materials with polished technical phrases, and a third steps forward to describe the acoustic details that make the lobby sound spacious without feeling cold. Everything flows with a natural ease that surprises me.

I don't step in. There's no need. I watch from the side, hands clasped, letting the building speak in its own language through other voices. And there, among the crowd, I notice Allison—smiling, Daniel beside her—listening to one of the hosts as if she were a guest herself. It's a relief to see her enjoying the moment, setting aside the weight of work and letting others take the lead.

The crowd spreads out into small groups. The stairs receive footsteps that previously existed only in my renderings; the corridors fill with murmurs that echo like improvised music. A woman stops just beneath the beam of light coming from the skylight—she closes her eyes for a moment, as if the light itself were a breath. In the lobby, a boy runs, fascinated by how the shadows seem to bend to his will.

I walk a few steps behind each group, not to guide them, but to observe. Every reaction reminds me why this building exists: not for my obsessions, but for others to experience, claim, and make it their own.

I stand still for a few seconds at the foot of the stairs, watching the guests begin to climb. They move slowly, as if each step were a discovery. Some look upward, tracing the curve of the wooden railing as it winds along the ascent; others run their fingertips along the smooth handrail, as though to confirm that it truly exists beyond a blueprint or model.

Conversations weave together in an eager murmur:

— "Look how the light comes in… it seems to change with every step."

— "Do you hear that? There's no echo, even though it's all open."

— "It's like being outside, but without the heat."

Their words catch in my chest. Each one reminds me that what I once sketched alone at my desk has become something real—something others can feel too.

Farther up, a man in a dark suit says to the woman beside him,

"This isn't a building... It's an experience."

And she answers, smiling as she adjusts her purse on her shoulder,

"It's exactly what he wanted."

I don't know if they were talking about me or if it was a coincidence, but those words hit with the quiet force of inevitability.

A group of architecture students, notebooks in hand, stops halfway up the stairs. One sketches quickly, trying to capture the curve and the diagonal shadows it casts. Another says softly,

"You couldn't copy this. You'd have to feel it to understand it."

I follow a few steps behind them, not stepping in. I want to listen, to hold on to those unfiltered words. The staircase—the one I measured so many times on paper—now breathes with their voices, their laughter, their gestures of wonder.

On the landings, people lean toward the windows, gazing out at the city stretching in the distance. I hear a quiet exclamation:

"It looks like even the view was designed."

And I think maybe it was—because from here, even the city feels like part of this place.

From afar, I spot Dave with Sarah and the kids, following one of the hosts down a side corridor. Emma stops in front of a stone wall and runs her hand along its surface, as if memorizing its texture. Lucas, meanwhile, hops from tile to tile, testing the echo of each step as if it were part of a game. Sarah smiles—calm, patient—and Dave watches them with that serene composure of his, never detached, always attentive, as if he wanted to absorb every detail to remember it later.

A few feet away, I catch sight of Allison holding Daniel's hand. He listens intently to the host explaining the logic of the design, while she lets out a soft laugh and corrects a detail, adding another of her own—as if even here she couldn't resist joining in.

Samuel follows behind another group, impeccable as always, answering technical questions with short, confident phrases that make visitors nod in understanding.

I watch them all and think that, in a way, this building already belongs to them too. They move through it with ease, as if the space had been waiting for them. And that, more than any applause, is what makes it real.

As I keep walking, taking in how they observe each corner, a metallic echo reaches me from the lobby speakers. It's not a formal call or an announcement—just a soft message over the microphone at the far end of the hall:

"Matthew Prescott, the podium is ready for you."

The murmur fades slowly, like the moment the wind stills the leaves. Every face turns toward me. Heat climbs up my neck, more suffocating than any tie. My hands are sweaty, and the jacket that already felt uncomfortable this morning now feels like armor—heavy and too stiff to move in.

I make my way slowly through the improvised rows of guests. There's no marked aisle, but their eyes make one. Some shake my hand as I pass, others give a quick pat on the shoulder; most simply smile, as if that's their way of saying "congratulations." I nod back, grateful but wordless.

Each step feels longer than it should. The lights, the hushed murmur, the flashes sparking in the distance—all of it seems to conspire to remind me that I've become the center of a scene I never sought.

When I reach the front, I see Allison waiting. She holds the microphone and gives me a calm, knowing smile, as if to say, "You can do it." There's no podium, no screen, no slides to deflect attention—just a slightly raised platform at the edge of the lobby, with a perfectly placed blue carpet. Minimalist. Intentional. Like everything in this building.

I climb the last step and feel the shift in perspective: every face lifts toward me again. I take a deep breath. The silence is so crisp it feels like another material in the design, as if the building itself had joined in the act of waiting for my words.

The microphone lets out a sharp squeal, and my heart pounds, ready to burst. One, two, three, four... I hold on to the rhythm like an invisible scaffold, then lift my gaze. Everyone is waiting. Now it's my turn to speak.

The silence stretches a few seconds longer than it should. I swallow, adjust my tie even though I know it couldn't be any tighter, and let out a breath that echoes softly through the microphone.

"I'll be honest..." I begin with a tense smile I can't quite hide. "I've never liked microphones. I've always preferred blueprints, renderings, and drawings. They never interrupt you, never wait for a joke—or a pause."

A ripple of quiet laughter rises from the crowd, just enough to loosen the invisible tie around my neck.

"Thank you... Thank you all for being here today." I glance around the full lobby, at the faces turned toward me. "I don't have many rehearsed words, because this day, more than speeches, calls for gratitude."

I pause, letting my eyes travel across the space: the light pouring in from the skylight, the gentle murmur of water on the wall, the shimmering reflections on the glass. Everything seems to speak for me, as if the building itself wants to say something in my place.

"I'll admit it still feels unreal to stand here. Years ago, this place existed only in my mind—in a notebook filled with crooked sketches and scribbled notes. Now I see it alive, full of voices and footsteps... and all I feel is gratitude."

I take a deep breath. The silence now isn't awkward—it's an accomplice.

"Welcome to this space. Welcome to what we dreamed, what we argued over a thousand times, what we raised through dust, coffee, and sleepless nights. Thank you for being here in this moment, which for me isn't just an inauguration—it's proof that when dreams are held up by many, they can become solid ground."

"I always dreamed that this space would be more than just offices."

My voice comes steadier now, as if the building itself were speaking with me. "I wanted it to embody what we believe in at Divergent Holdings—that architecture doesn't just shield us from the weather or organize square meters, but that it can create a sense of belonging."

I look around, letting the pause speak for me.

"It was important that the home of our company said that—with every wall, every shadow, every gesture. That here, in this lobby, anyone—whether they work here or simply visit—can feel there's a place that welcomes them, that includes them."

I make a slight motion toward the skylight, toward the silent flow of water.

"This building is how I've chosen to say: this is how we see the world—with transparency, with roots, with spaces that breathe. This is how we want to work. This is how we want to live."

Applause breaks like a wave that rises and folds over me—hands thundering on the marble floors, voices swelling in an improvised chorus, flashes crackling as if trying to capture every second. The lobby vibrates with the energy of everyone present, and I breathe deeply to contain it. I let the pride of the moment carry me, even as it feels larger inside than I can hold in my hands.

I lift my hand slightly—a discreet, almost shy gesture—to invite the noise to fade. Gradually, the clapping softens, and the silence returns, wrapping around us, waiting. I breathe in, feel the heat still at my neck, and let gratitude push the following words forward.

"Thank you," I say at last, my voice low enough that everyone leans in to hear. "Thank you for being here. This isn't just a building or an opening ceremony. It's the sum of many hands, many voices, debates, calculations, long nights."

I glance toward them—the ones closest to me.

"I want to thank those who walked every step with me:

Allison—your strategic vision, your way of balancing what see-med impossible.

Samuel—your precision, your calm when the numbers refused to add up.

Dave—your friendship, your words when the weight felt too heavy… and your family, who constantly remind me what home truly means.

And to everyone whose effort and hands made this building rise."

I let their names breathe in the air.

"This space was born from a dream, yes—but it stood because of you. That's why today, this building carries not just my imprint, but the mark of everyone who made it possible."

I draw a slow breath. I can feel my words nearing their end—and with them, the moment everyone has been waiting for.

"Today, this building officially receives its name."

I pause, letting the air settle, letting the silence take its shape.

"A name that holds what was once a dream, what we defended together, what has now become reality."

At the back of the lobby, the blue covering begins to slip downward. The sound is barely audible, but the entire crowd seems to hold its breath, part of the ritual itself. The covering falls softly, without drama, revealing the polished steel letters behind it—tall, refined, catching the light with a quiet brilliance that needs no embellishment.

Divergent One.

A soft wave of voices swept through the crowd. Some voices repeated the name in whispers, testing it on their lips, letting it settle. Applause followed—steady, full, filling the entire space.

I keep my eyes on the letters a moment longer. To anyone else, they're just metal, well-designed typography. To me, they are years of doubt, of dust on my clothes, of nights counting to four just to keep from breaking. Seeing them anchored to the wall stirs an impossible mix: pride and vertigo, as if the building itself were reminding me that dreams grow heavy once they become real.

Behind the letters, the stone wall awakens. A thread of water begins to fall—tentative at first, as if testing its path—until it becomes a smooth cascade, clear and bright under the light. The water slips down and frames the freshly revealed name, as though baptizing it in that very instant.

The whispers join the applause, a deep, continuous sound that fills the lobby with calm, reminding everyone that this place stands not only on steel and concrete, but also on movement—on life.

I allow myself the faintest smile, just enough for Allison to catch my gaze from the side, her eyes glinting with that spark of shared triumph.

And I think: yes, now Divergent One is no longer mine. It belongs to everyone.

The applause rolled on like an unbroken tide, and I tell myself: it's time to accept it. Don't step back, don't diminish it. It's for me, yes—but also for my team, for every hand that shaped this dream. I look at the people clapping, some standing, others smiling with genuine warmth, and for the first time, I let that energy move through me without resistance. And I feel it—the emotion of receiving, the quiet certainty that this moment is mine too.

The lobby begins to empty, little by little. Footsteps fade like receding waves; voices thin into distant echoes. A pair of assistants removes chairs, others fold up cables, and pack away microphones. The water on the wall keeps running, steady and self-contained, as if what just happened didn't quite belong to it. The artificial light glints softly on the marble, and for an instant the space feels mine again—or almost.

I'm not alone. Beside me are Allison, Daniel, Samuel, and Dave with his family. Emma walks barefoot across the marble as if testing its cool texture; Lucas plays with the shadows of his own hands while Sarah watches him, smiling. Allison laughs softly, still holding Daniel's hand, and Samuel stands tall with that calm demeanor that never leaves him. Dave looks at me with that expression of his—a mix of solemnity and mischief—and breaks the silence.

"Enough of the ceremony," he says. "Time to celebrate for real. What do you say, Matt? Is your secret spot waiting for us?"

Allison bursts out laughing, as if she'd known he would say that. Samuel nods wordlessly, a small gesture that says he's in. I stay quiet for a second, smiling. I've always thought of that place as mine—a refuge I never needed to share. But today... Today feels different.

"Let's go," I say. "It's the perfect day for it."

The restaurant welcomes us with its usual familiarity—the soft lights, the scent of wood, and the aroma of toasted bread. Behind the bar, James spots me the moment I walk in, but this time I go over only to greet him. Before I can say anything, Dave speaks up, his voice warm and easy.

"James, we're all together today. It's a day to celebrate. Get us a big table—one that can hold all our stories."

James smiles as if he'd been waiting for this. He nods and leads us to a spotless table: the linens crisp, the glasses waiting, a corner made for conversation.

We settle in. Emma gives us her version of the day, embellishing every detail as though it were a fairy tale. Lucas folds the napkins into clumsy shapes and sets them in front of us like improvised gifts. Allison laughs softly; Daniel listens, captivated. Samuel raises his glass with few words but clear intent: "To what we've achieved." Dave jumps in with stories that make us all laugh, and Sarah anchors the moment with her unshakable calm.

I look at them. I listen to the voices, the laughter, the interruptions, the spontaneous toasts. And I realize—I'm not standing at the edge anymore, not watching from a distance. I'm inside it, part of the table, part of the story. Maybe belonging isn't more complicated than this: to sit, to listen, to laugh, to let life be shared without measuring the silences.

Dave lifts his glass again. There's no speech prepared, only the honest spark in his eyes.

"To Divergent One... but more than that, to us."

The glasses rise. Laughter and voices mingle in a simple, unplanned, perfect toast. I raise mine and smile. This time there's no vertigo, no hesitation—only the quiet certainty that I am exactly where I'm meant to be.

Humberto M. Sotomayor

Epilogue

Light enters slowly through the window, barely hinting at the day. There's no alarm, no urgency; the house breathes in calm, as if it too knows it's Sunday. Everything moves at a slower rhythm—the air, the wooden floor beneath my feet, even the clock in the living room seems to fall behind in a conspiratorial way. Outside, the city begins to stir timidly, but here, time stretches, as if trying to gift me a few more hours of silence.

The smell of coffee lingers in the kitchen, fresh and still hot. I pour it into my usual mug and carry it with me—not to drink right away, but like someone holding a charm. The steam rises slowly, forming shapes that vanish in the air, and I find myself following them with my gaze, as if they were ephemeral drawings someone had traced just for me.

I dress without ceremony: jeans, a black T-shirt, and comfortable sneakers. Nothing tight, nothing that shines too much. No tie or suit today; no stage, only the simplicity of being myself again. In the mirror, my reflection returns a quiet image—not the polished figure from yesterday, but something closer, more honest. I run a hand through my hair and smile with a hint of irony. Sometimes I think true elegance lies in being yourself—without disguise.

Toby stretches in his little bed—custom-made, surrounded by the stuffed animals he's claimed as his over the years. He gets up, takes a few steps, and follows me with his slow, sleepy gait. He shakes his ears and tilts his head, watching me as if to ask where I'm going this time. I scratch behind his head, sinking my fingers into his warm fur. That simple touch brings me back to earth. It's remarkable how a dog's loyalty can make you feel accompanied, even in the most extended silences.

I walk toward the door with my keys in hand, but something stops me. It isn't haste or forgetfulness—it's the quiet certainty that something's missing. I retrace my steps, climb back to the room, and open the nightstand drawer. There it is, waiting as always: the notebook. The binding is bent out of shape; its pages bear stains, folds, and scars from use. But in every page lives a piece of me—the sketches of imagined buildings, the words I never said aloud, the ill-timed calculations, the invisible maps my mind insisted on keeping.

I pick it up carefully, like someone lifting a secret. I run my thumb along the edge, checking without opening it that everything essential is still there—everything I can't leave behind. I tuck it under my arm. This time, it's coming with me; I know it needs to go with me today.

Back in the living room, Toby watches me from his bed, and for a moment I feel his gaze on me—patient, almost waiting for permission to sleep again. I lean down, scratch behind his ears once more, and his eyes close at once, trusting.

"I'll be back soon, little buddy," I whisper. "You know I always come back."

I close the door behind me. There are no crowds, no applause—only a quiet street, carrying the scent of damp grass and cool asphalt. I take a deep breath, letting the sigh fill me, and think that maybe this day needs nothing more than this: a forgotten cup of coffee, a resting dog, a notebook under my arm.

I drive without hurry. The city still seems asleep: a few early runners, shutters lifting, a truck unloading boxes in front of a shop. Everything looks routine, and yet, for me, every green light feels like a quiet gesture of complicity.

When I turn the last corner, the building comes into view. No longer a construction site, no longer a stage for applause—just what it is: a place waiting for me. I take the ramp down into the underground parking lot, my new arrival point. From today on, this will be my place, my routine: drive down, park, go up, live it. I pull into what will be my new spot. I don't need to look at the painted lines on the ground; my body already knows the angle, the curve, the precision of each maneuver.

I close the door, and the metallic echo rings louder than it should in a space so vast, as if solitude itself amplifies sound. Heading toward the elevator, I see my steps reflected on the polished floor, and for a moment, I catch myself as a visitor, not an architect. I press the button; a small orange circle glows under my finger. The elevator answers at once—a smooth glide, no harsh sound, as if even its motion wished to remain discreet.

When the doors open, the lobby greets me differently than it did on inauguration day. No voices, no cameras, no laughter bouncing off the walls. Only the steady flow of water down the stone wall and the light that falls in diagonals from the skylight. Together, they're enough to fill the space. The marble returns a soft shimmer; each shadow moves with the building's own rhythm, as if it were breathing in silence.

I walk unhurriedly, hands in my pockets, letting my footsteps fade into the echo. The furniture is in perfect order—the chairs aligned, the tables clean—as if someone had left everything ready for a performance that hasn't yet begun. I think how beautiful it looks like

215

this, stripped of noise, reduced to its essence: light, water, stone, air—a refuge without witnesses.

The security guard greets me from the entrance with a slight nod.

"Good morning, Architect," he says softly, almost as if afraid to disturb the calm.

I answer with a slight smile.

"Good morning, Robert."

Nothing more is needed. His presence reassures me—someone is watching over this place even when I'm not here, as if the building itself had its own guardian.

I climb the central staircase. The wooden handrail feels warm beneath my palm, and each step reminds me of all the times I imagined it in sketches, in renderings, in endless discussions about proportions. Now it's here, holding me without hesitation. From the landing, I stop and look down: the lobby appears like a stage seen from above, with the water flowing like a perpetual curtain.

I walk through the corridors and step into the office that will now be mine. Everything is in its place: the broad desk, the empty shelves waiting to be filled with books and blueprints, the window framing the city as if it were a living painting. I run my hand over the smooth surface of the desk, and for a moment, I imagine the coffee stains, the wrinkled pages, the urgent sketches that will soon cover it. It doesn't bother me—on the contrary, I know it will mean the space has begun to be used, to live.

The building isn't empty, I think. It's at rest. There's a difference: emptiness is absence; rest is readiness. Today, I walk through it in that state, like someone listening to an instrument tuning before the music begins.

I head for the rooftop. The elevator rises calmly, and when the doors open, the light hits me full on. The city unfolds before me—avenues pulsing in the distance, rooftops gleaming under the sun, a horizon that seems to have no end. I walk to one of the tables near the railing and sit down. The air moves gently, carrying the scent of warm concrete and open sky. I set the notebook on the table, rest my palm on it as if claiming a private territory, and let the breeze stir my hair while I prepare to write.

The black cover is worn at the corners, bearing traces of having been too many places with me—noisy restaurants, meeting rooms, impersonal hotel desks, even my own kitchen table on sleepless nights. I open it and run my fingers over the filled pages. The blue ink repeats itself line after line, as if every word were an attempt to arrange the noise in my head.

I pick up the pen. The cold metal settles between my fingers, and it surprises me that even after all these years of writing, my hand still trembles slightly in this moment. It isn't the tremor of doubt, but of significance. Today, in this place, I feel that every word will be anchored to the building itself, as if stone and paper shared the same memory.

I write slowly.

> *"I understood that this building no longer belongs to me. I dreamed it, drew it, defended it. But now it lives in the eyes of others, in their steps, in their voices. It belongs to those who inhabit it."*

I pause. The wind moves over the pages, lifting them slightly, as if it were trying to read ahead of time. I smile and write another line.

> *"Maybe building was never about steel or concrete, but about the*

possibility that someone might find here a place where they can recognize themselves."

I lift my gaze. From the rooftop, the city pulses. Cars look like tiny insects crawling through asphalt arteries. The neighboring towers throw flashes of light that make me squint. And in the midst of that immensity, here I am—with a notebook and a pen—trying to catch what I feel in clumsy but necessary lines.

I keep writing.

"For years, I thought my mind was condemned to measure, to count, to calculate. Today I've learned it can also let go. That belonging doesn't mean fitting perfectly, but allowing others to sit at the table with you."

I smile again. The echo of last night's dinner—Allison, Daniel, Samuel, Dave, Sarah, the children—returns like a warm wave. I hear the laughter, the overlapping voices, the spontaneous toasts. I write:

"It isn't the building that sustains me. It's the people who stood with me to raise it."

The wind grows stronger. I place my palm over the page to keep it from closing. I think of the child I once was, drawing impossible houses with crayons on crumpled sheets of paper. If I could speak to him now, I'd tell him: "Not all your lines will be straight; not all your blueprints will be built. But some will. And those few will be enough to make you smile one day, knowing it was worth it."

I write the last line slowly, as if I wanted to carve it into the page—and into myself:

"I'll keep writing. Not to understand everything, because maybe I never will, but because in these pages, at least, I belong."

I close the notebook gently. The sound is soft, yet it moves through me like an intimate applause. I set the pen on top and lean back in the chair, letting the wind muss my hair again. Somewhere in the building, water flows; its murmur reaches up here, blending with the steady breath of the breeze.

I stay that way for a few minutes, watching the city. Behind me, the building beats like something newly alive. In front of me, the notebook holds its written memory. And for the first time in a long while, there's no urgency in me now—only calm.

Humberto M. Sotomayor

Gratitude

What would this book be without all the people who have stood by me throughout my life? Without those who have inspired me, taught me, and helped me overcome my own fears and weaknesses.

I want to thank, first and foremost, my family—my father, my mother, my sister, and my niece. Though we are far from a perfect family, it was they who laid the foundations of my life.

I also want to thank all my collaborators, who made it possible for me to find the time to write these pages.

To Cuauhtémoc, for his wisdom and patience.

To Dariana, for her spark, her dedication, and her kindness, which continue to inspire me despite her youth.

To Paola, my first accomplice in reading my drafts.

To Julio, who appeared without my looking for him—a friend who listens, accepts, and understands me.

To Joel and Roberto, who are always there.

To the friends from my youth, still part of my life, who somehow always appear when I need them most.

To Rex, the most loyal of all, who taught me more about belonging than any book ever could, and with whom I shared much of my life—now watching me from heaven.

And to Max, playful and bright, who fills my solitary spaces with joy.

I also want to thank, with no less gratitude, Dr. Nelson, who helped me see that my weaknesses carry more light than shadow. And

Bárbara, who helped me find, in the deepest of myself, the feelings I had long refused to bring into the light.

I would not have come this far without the relationships time has given me—the failures that turned into lessons, the joyful and painful moments that, together, have shaped my character.

I want to thank God, life, and the universe for giving me the chance to live… and to find a way to express myself through these pages.

And to all of you—thank you. This book also belongs to you.

Humberto M. Sotomayor

www.ingramcontent.com/pod-product-compliance
Lightning Source LLC
Chambersburg PA
CBHW022140240626
47153CB00007B/2441